"Which bed would you prefer?"

Sloane regarded her thoughtfully. "You don't want to share?"

"No," Suzanne told him. She didn't want to think about it, didn't *dare*. It was bad enough having to share the same villa, the same bedroom!

To share the same bed was definitely impossible. Unless she was into casual sex, for the sake of sex. And she wasn't. To her, sex meant intimacy, sensuality, *love*.

"A word of warning, Suzanne," Sloane said softly. "Don't expect me to behave like a gentleman."

Anything can happen behind closed doors!

Do you dare find out…?

Welcome to the final book in our sizzling, sensual
miniseries DO NOT DISTURB!

Meet the last of four different couples thrown
together by circumstances into a whirlwind of
unexpected attraction. Forced into each other's
company whether they like it or not, they're soon in
the grip of passion—and definitely *don't* want to
be disturbed!

This month it's the turn of popular Presents™ author
Helen Bianchin to explore this delicious fantasy in a
tantalizing romance you simply won't want to
put down.

What happens when Suzanne and her ex-fiancé
Sloane find themselves sharing **The Bridal Bed**…?
Turn the pages and find out!

HELEN BIANCHIN

The Bridal Bed

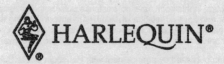

HARLEQUIN®

TORONTO • NEW YORK • LONDON
AMSTERDAM • PARIS • SYDNEY • HAMBURG
STOCKHOLM • ATHENS • TOKYO • MILAN • MADRID
PRAGUE • WARSAW • BUDAPEST • AUCKLAND

ISBN 0-373-11996-8

THE BRIDAL BED

First North American Publication 1998.

Copyright © 1998 by Helen Bianchin.

This edition published by arrangement with Harlequin Books S.A.

® and TM are trademarks of the publisher. Trademarks indicated with
® are registered in the United States Patent and Trademark Office, the
Canadian Trade Marks Office and in other countries.

Printed in U.S.A.

CHAPTER ONE

It SHOULD be Friday the thirteenth, Suzanne determined as she perused the perfectly printed legal document on her desk and noted yet another clause she knew wasn't worded to her client's best interest.

Midwinter had delivered metropolitan Sydney with a shocking day, and she'd woken to howling winds and heavy rain. Consequently she'd got wet traversing the external stairs leading from her tiny Manly flat down to the garage beneath.

Her car, which had up until now behaved impeccably, had decided not to start. A telephone call to the automobile association had elicited there was a backlog of calls, and it would be at least an hour before someone could come to her rescue. Two hours later the diagnosis had been a dead battery, and it had taken a further hour to organise a replacement and drive into the city.

Consequently she'd been late, very late arriving at the inner-city legal office where she worked as one of several junior solicitors. A fact that hadn't sat well with two waiting clients who had been virtuously punctual. Nor had the senior partner been very happy that she'd missed an important staff meeting.

There had been files piled up on her desk, messages that required attention, and three rescheduled appointments lined up one after the other. Lunch hadn't even been an option.

Mid-afternoon came and went as she struggled to catch up on a workload that threatened to spill over into work she would have to take home.

'Suzanne, urgent call on line three.' The receptionist's voice sounded hesitant, diffident, and vaguely apologetic for breaching a 'hold all calls' instruction. 'It's your mother.'

Her mother *never* rang her at work. An icy hand clutched Suzanne's heart as she snatched up the receiver. 'Georgia? Is something wrong?'

A light, husky laugh echoed down the line. 'Darling, everything's fine. It's just that I wanted you to be the first to hear my news.'

'*News*, Mama?' She kept her voice deliberately light. 'You've won a fabulous prize? Bought a new car? Booked an overseas trip?'

There was a breathless pause. 'Right on two counts.'

'Which two?'

'Well, sweetheart,' Georgia began with a delicious chuckle, 'the overseas trip is booked...*Paris*, would you believe? And I *have* won a fabulous prize.'

'That's wonderful.' Really wonderful. Suzanne shook her head in silent amazement. Georgia was always taking lottery and raffle tickets, but had never won anything other than the most minor of prizes until now.

'It's not exactly a *prize* prize.'

The faintly cautious tone had Suzanne sinking back

in her chair. 'You're talking in riddles, Mama. Is there a catch to any of this?'

'No catch. At least, not the kind you mean.'

What had her cautious mother got herself into? 'I'm listening.'

'Bear with me, darling.' Georgia's voice hitched, then raced on in an excited rush. 'It's all so new, I still have a hard time believing it. And I wouldn't have rung you at work, except I really couldn't wait a minute longer.'

'*Tell me.*'

There was silence for a few seconds. 'I'm getting married.'

Initial joy was quickly followed by concern, and it was a frightening mix. Her mother didn't *date*. There was a collection of friends, but no *one* man. 'I didn't know you were seeing anyone,' Suzanne said slowly, and heard her mother's light laughter in response. 'Who is he, and where did you meet him?'

'We met at your engagement party, darling.'

Three months. They'd only known each other three months. 'Who, Mama?'

'Trenton Wilson-Willoughby. Sloane's father.'

Oh, my God. Heat rushed through her veins, then chilled to ice. 'You're not serious?' Tell me you're not serious, she pleaded silently.

'You sound—shocked,' Georgia responded slowly, and Suzanne quickly gathered her wits.

Recoup, regroup, *fast*. 'Surprised,' she amended. 'It seems so sudden.'

'Sometimes love happens that way. Sloane swept you off your feet in a matter of weeks.'

Like father, like son. 'Yes,' she agreed cautiously. Sloane had gifted her a sparkling diamond, whisked her down to Sydney from Brisbane, and moved her into his Rose Bay penthouse apartment before she'd had time to think, let alone catch her breath. Blinded by a riveting attraction and primitive alchemy.

'When is the wedding taking place?' A few months from now would give her plenty of time to—what? Explain that she was no longer living with Sloane?

'This weekend, darling.' Georgia sounded vaguely breathless and tremendously excited.

This weekend. Today was *Wednesday*, for heaven's sake. 'Don't you think—?'

'It's a bit sudden?' her mother finished. 'Yes, darling, I do. But Trenton is a very convincing man.'

Suzanne took a deep breath, then released it slowly. 'You're quite sure about this?'

'As sure as I can be.' There was a funny catch in her voice. 'Aren't you going to congratulate me?'

Oh, *hell.* She had to collect her thoughts together. 'Of course I am. And give you my blessing. I'm just so happy *you* are happy.' She was babbling, she knew, but she couldn't stop. 'Where is the wedding taking place? Have you chosen what you'll wear?'

Georgia began to laugh, and, Suzanne suspected, to cry. 'Bedarra Island, Saturday afternoon. Would you believe Trenton has booked all the accommodation on the island to ensure total privacy? I'm wearing a cream silk suit, with matching shoes and hat. We want you and Sloane to be witnesses.'

Bedarra Island was a privately owned resort situated high in North Queensland's Whitsunday group of tropical islands. A minimum three-hour flight, followed by a launch trip to Bedarra.

'Trenton has organised for you both to fly up on Friday morning and stay until Monday.'

Oh, my. Trenton's organisation would include the family jet, the charter of a private launch.

Sloane.

It was three weeks since she'd walked out of his apartment, leaving a penned note briefly spelling out her need for some time alone. It attributed nothing to the reality of an anonymous threat if she didn't end the engagement.

A threat she hadn't taken seriously until the young socialite who'd initiated it had almost run Suzanne's car off the road to emphasise her intent, then identified herself and promised grievous bodily harm if Suzanne failed to comply.

The sequence of events had been very carefully planned, she reflected, to coincide with Sloane's absence overseas. Bitter, vitriolic invective had merely added doubt as to the socialite's mental stability, and extreme caution had motivated Suzanne to leave Sloane's apartment and move all her clothes into a flat on the other side of the city.

However, she had underestimated Sloane. When she'd refused to take his calls on his return, he'd pulled rank and walked unannounced into her office.

His icy anger when she had refused to elaborate on the contents of her note had been so chilling, it had been all she could do not to fall in a heap the second the door had closed behind him.

Now it appeared she had little option but to see him again.

Suzanne slowly replaced the receiver, then stared sightlessly at the wall in front of her. Georgia and Trenton. Could her mother possibly guess at the complications she'd created?

Allowing no time for hesitation, Suzanne punched in the digit to access an outside line, then completed the set of numbers that would connect with Sloane's law chambers.

Not that the call did much good. All she received was a relayed message stating that Sloane Wilson-Willoughby was in court and wasn't expected back until late afternoon. Suzanne logged in her name and phone number on his message bank.

Damn. The silent curse did little to ease her frustration as she turned her attention to the documents requiring her perusal. She made a note of two clauses she felt were not entirely to her client's advantage, pencilled in a notation to delete one, and re-phrase another. Then she had her secretary lodge the necessary call in order to apprise the client of her suggested alterations.

The afternoon was hectic, and the nerves inside her stomach became increasingly tense as the minutes ticked by. Each time the phone rang, she mentally

prepared herself for it to be Sloane, only to have her
secretary announce someone else.

Was he deliberately delaying the call? Just to make
her sweat a little? Whatever, it was playing havoc
with her nervous system.

At five her phone buzzed just as she ushered a client from her office, and she crossed to her desk and
picked up the receiver.

'Sloane Wilson-Willoughby on line two.' The information was imparted in a faintly breathless voice,
and Suzanne momentarily raised her eyes towards the
ceiling.

Sloane tended to have that effect on people.
Women, especially, responded to something in his
deep, smoky voice. Once they sighted him in the
flesh, the response went into overdrive and tended to
make vamps and vixens out of the most sensible of
females.

She should know. She'd been there herself. Part of
her ached for the promise, the dream of what they
might have had together.

Then she drew in a deep breath, released it, and
picked up the receiver. 'Sloane.' To ask 'how are
you?' seemed incredibly banal.

'Suzanne.' The polite acknowledgement seared
something deep inside, and she resolutely kept her
voice even as she sank back in her chair. 'Georgia
rang me. I believe Trenton has relayed their news?'

'Yes.' Brief, succinct, and unforthcoming.

He wasn't making it easy for her. There was no

way out of this, and it was best if she just got on with it.

'We need to talk.'

'I agree,' Sloane indicated silkily. 'Make it dinner tonight.' He named a restaurant in a city hotel. 'Seven.'

She needed to put in another hour in order to appease her employer. 'I don't think—'

'It's the restaurant or your flat.' His voice acquired the sound of silk being razed by steel. 'Choose.'

She didn't hesitate. 'Seven-thirty.' A public place where there were people was the lesser of two evils. The thought of Sloane appearing at her flat, demanding entry...

'Wise.'

No, it was most *unwise*, but she didn't appear to have much option.

Suzanne replaced the receiver and attempted to concentrate on notations she needed to finalise.

Consequently it was well after six when she left the office, and almost seven before she reached home.

Within half an hour she'd showered, dressed, swept her damp hair into a sleek twist, applied make-up with practised precision, and she was on her way out of the door, retracing a familiar route into the city.

Except this time the traffic was more civilised. And there was the advantage of valet parking. Even so, she was fifteen minutes late.

Suzanne pushed open the heavy glass door and entered the hotel lobby. It took only seconds to locate a familiar dark-suited figure standing several metres distant.

Her pulse tripped its beat and accelerated to a faster pace as she watched him unfold his lengthy frame from a deep-cushioned lounge chair.

Sloane Wilson-Willoughby stood four inches over six feet, with the broad shoulders and muscled frame of a superbly trained athlete. Inherited genes had bestowed ruggedly attractive facial features, piercing brown eyes, and thick dark brown hair. Evident was an aura of power, and the ease of a man well versed in the strengths and weaknesses of his fellow men.

He watched as she moved towards him, his appraisal swift, taking in the red power suit adorning her petite frame, the upswept hairstyle and the stiletto heels she invariably wore to add inches to her height. She possessed an innate femininity that was at variance with the professional image she tried so hard to maintain. Slight but very feminine curves, slender, shapely legs, silken-smooth honey-gold skin, deep blue eyes, and a mouth to die for.

He'd tasted its delights, savoured the pleasures of her body, and put an engagement ring on her finger. It had stayed there precisely ten weeks before she'd taken it off with an excuse he'd no more believed then than he did now.

'Sloane.' She moved forward and accepted the touch of his hand at her elbow. And told herself she was impervious to the clean male smell of him mingling with the faint aroma of his exclusive brand of cologne. Immune to the latent sensuality that seemed to emanate from every pore.

He searched her pale features, and noted the faint smudges beneath eyes that seemed too large for her face. 'Working hard?'

The deceptive mildness of his voice didn't fool her in the slightest. She effected a light shrug and opted for flippancy. 'Next you'll tell me I've dropped weight.'

He lifted a hand and traced her jawline with his thumb. And saw her eyes dilate. 'Two or three essential kilos, at a guess.'

His touch was like fire, and a muscle flickered in involuntary reaction. 'Judge, advocate and jury rolled into one?'

'Lover,' Sloane amended.

'Ex-lover,' she corrected him, and saw the sensual curve of his lower lip.

'Your choice, not mine.'

She deliberately moved back a pace, and met his gaze squarely. 'Shall we go in to dinner?'

'You wouldn't prefer a drink first?'

She really wanted to keep this as short as possible. 'No.' She sought to qualify her decision. 'I really can't stay long.'

There was a tinge of wry humour evident in his voice as they walked towards the bank of lifts. 'Dedication to duty, Suzanne?'

The humour stung. 'Suffice it to say it's been one of those days, and I have work to catch up on.'

A set of doors slid open and she preceded him into

the lift. They were the only occupants, and he leaned forward to depress the button for the appropriate floor.

His suit sleeve brushed against her arm, and she tried to ignore the shivery sensation feathering over her skin. Her fine body hairs rose in protective self-defence, and she felt her pulse trip and surge to a faster beat.

Did he realise he still had this effect on her? Probably not, she reassured herself silently, for she strove very hard to project detached disinterest.

The restaurant was well patronised, and the *maître d'* led them to a reserved table, saw them seated, and summoned the drinks waiter.

Suzanne viewed the menu with interest, and she ordered soup *du jour*, a seafood starter, and grilled fish as a main course.

'Do we attempt to engage in polite conversation,' Sloane drawled as soon as the waiter disappeared, 'or shall we cut straight to the chase?'

Suzanne forced herself to hold his gaze. 'Dinner was your idea.'

Evident was the leashed anger beneath his control. 'What did you expect? A curt directive to meet me at the airport Friday morning?'

'Yes.'

His smile was totally without humour. 'Ah, *honesty*.'

'It's one of my more admirable traits.'

Their drinks were delivered, and Suzanne sipped the iced water, almost wishing it were something stronger. Alcohol might soothe her fractured nerves.

She watched as Sloane took an appreciative swallow of his customary spritzer before setting the glass onto the table, then leaning back in his chair.

'You haven't responded to any of my messages.'

It was difficult to retain his gaze, but she managed. 'There didn't seem much point.'

'I beg to differ.'

He was a skilled wordsmith and a brilliant strategist. He was also icy calm. When all he wanted to do was reach forward and *shake* her.

'We're here to discuss our respective parents' marriage to each other,' she managed civilly. 'Not conduct a post-mortem on our affair.'

'Post-mortem?' His voice was a sibilant threat. *'Affair?'*

He was playing with her, much as a predatory animal played with its prey. Waiting, watching, assessing each and every move, in no doubt of the kill. It was just a matter of *when*.

Suzanne rose to her feet and reached for her bag. 'I've had one hell of a day. I have work to get through when I get home.' Her eyes flashed angrily. 'I don't need you playing cat-and-mouse with me.'

A hand closed over her arm, and it took all her control not to shake it free.

'Sit down.'

She would have liked nothing better than to turn and walk out of the door. But there was Georgia to consider. No matter how difficult the weekend might prove to be, she *had* to be present at her mother's wedding. Anything else was unthinkable.

'Please,' Sloane added, and without a word she sank down into her chair.

Almost on cue the waiter delivered their soup, and she spooned it slowly, grateful for the ensuing silence.

When their plates were removed she picked up her glass and sipped the contents.

'Tell me about your day,' Sloane commanded with studied ease.

Suzanne looked at him carefully. 'Genuine interest, or an adept attempt to keep our conversation on an even keel?'

'Both.'

His faint, mocking smile was almost her undoing, and she felt like screaming with vexation. 'I'd prefer to discuss the weekend.'

'Indulge me. We have yet to begin the main course.'

At this rate she'd suffer indigestion. As it was, her stomach seemed to be tied in numerous knots.

'The car refused to start, the automobile club took ages to send someone out, I was late in to work, and I got soaked in the rain.' She effected a light shrug. 'That about encapsulates it.'

'I'll organise for you to have the use of one of my cars while yours is being checked out.'

A surge of anger rose to the surface. 'No. You won't.'

'Now you're being stubborn,' he drawled hatefully.

'Practical.' And wary of being seen driving his Porsche or Jaguar.

'Stubborn,' Sloane reiterated.

'You sound like my mother,' Suzanne responded with a deliberately slow, sweet smile.

'Heaven forbid.'

Anger rose once more, and her eyes assumed a fiery sparkle. 'You disapprove of Georgia?'

'Of being compared to anything vaguely *parental* where you're concerned,' Sloane corrected her with ill-concealed mockery.

Suzanne looked at him carefully, then honed a verbal dart. 'I doubt you've ever lacked a solitary thing in your privileged life.'

One eyebrow rose, and there was a certain wryness apparent. 'Except for the love of a good woman?'

'Most women fall over themselves to get to you,' she stated with marked cynicism.

'To the social prestige the Wilson-Willoughby name carries,' Sloane amended drily. 'And let's not forget the family wealth.'

The multi-million-dollar family home with its incredible views over Sydney harbour, the fleet of luxurious cars, servants. Not to mention Sloane's penthouse apartment, *his* cars. Homes, apartments in major European cities. The family cruiser, the family jet.

And then there was Wilson-Willoughby, headed by Trenton and notably one of Sydney's leading law firms. One had only to enter its exclusive portals, see the expensive antique furniture gracing every office, the original artwork on the walls, to appreciate the elegance of limitless wealth.

'You're a cynic.'

His expression didn't change. 'A realist.'

Their starter arrived, and Suzanne took her time savouring the delicate texture of the prawns in a superb sauce many a chef would kill to reproduce.

'Now that you've had some food, perhaps you'd like a glass of wine?'

And have it go straight to her head? 'Half a glass,' she qualified, and determined to sip it slowly during the main course.

'I hear you've taken on a very challenging brief,' she said.

Sloane pressed the napkin to the edge of his mouth, then discarded it down onto the damask-covered table. 'News travels fast.'

As did anything attached to Sloane Wilson-Willoughby. In or out of the courtroom.

He part-filled her glass with wine, then set it back in the ice bucket, dismissing the wine steward who appeared with apologetic deference.

Their main course arrived, and Suzanne admired the superbly presented fish and artistically displayed vegetable portions. It seemed almost a sacrilege to disturb the arrangement, and she forked delicate mouthfuls with enjoyment.

'Am I to understand Georgia meets with your approval as a prospective stepmother?'

Sloane viewed her with studied ease. She looked more relaxed, and her cheeks bore a slight colour. 'Georgia is a charming woman. I'm sure she and my father will be very happy together.'

The deceptive mildness of his tone brought forth a

musing smile. 'I would have to say the same about Trenton.'

Sloane lifted his glass and took a sip of wine, then regarded her thoughtfully over the rim. 'The question remains… What do you want to do about us?'

Her stomach executed a painful backflip. 'What do you mean, what do I want to do about *us*?'

The waiter arrived to remove their plates, then delivered a platter of fresh fruit, added a bowl of freshly whipped cream, and withdrew.

'Unless you've told Georgia differently, our respective parents believe we're living in pre-nuptial bliss,' Sloane relayed with deliberate patience. 'Do we spend the weekend pretending we're still together? Or do you want to spoil their day by telling them we're living apart?'

She didn't want to think about *together*. It merely heightened memories she longed to forget. Fat chance, a tiny voice taunted.

Fine clothes did little to tame a body honed to the height of physical fitness, or lessen his brooding sensuality. Too many nights she'd lain awake remembering just how it felt to be held in those arms, kissed in places she'd never thought to grant a licence to, and taught to scale unbelievable heights with a man who knew every path, every journey.

'Your choice, Suzanne.'

She looked at him and glimpsed the implacability beneath the charming façade, the velvet-encased steel.

As a barrister in a court of law he was skilled with the command of words and their delivery. She'd seen him in action, and been enthralled. Mesmerised. And had known, even then, that she'd have reason to quake if ever he became her enemy.

A game of pretence, and she wondered why she was even considering it. Yet would it be so bad?

There wasn't much choice if she didn't want to spoil her mother's happiness. The truth was something she intended to keep to herself.

'I imagine it isn't possible to fly in and out of Bedarra on the same day?'

'No.'

It was a slim hope, given the distance and the time of the wedding. 'There are no strings you can pull?'

'Afraid to spend time with me, Suzanne?' Sloane queried smoothly.

'I'd prefer to keep it to a minimum,' she said with innate honesty. 'And you didn't answer the question.'

'What strings would you have me pull?'

'It would be more suitable to arrive on Bedarra Saturday morning, and return Sunday.'

'And disappoint Trenton and Georgia?' He lifted his glass and took an appreciative swallow of excellent vintage wine. 'Did it occur to you that perhaps Georgia might need your help and moral support *before* the wedding?'

It made sense, Suzanne conceded. 'Surely we could return on Sunday?'

'I think not.'

'*Why?*'

He set the glass down onto the table with the utmost care. 'Because *I* won't be returning until Monday.'

She looked at him with a feeling of helpless anger. 'You're deliberately making this as difficult as possible, aren't you?'

'Trenton has organised to leave Sydney on Friday and return on Monday. I see no reason to disrupt those arrangements.'

A tiny shiver feathered its way down her spine.

Three days. Well, four if you wanted to be precise. Could she go through with it?

'Do you want to renege, Suzanne?'

The silkily voiced query strengthened her resolve, and her eyes speared his. 'No.'

'Can I interest you in the dessert trolley?'

The waiter's appearance was timely, and Suzanne turned her attention to the collection of delicious confections presented, and selected an utterly sinful slice of chocolate cake decorated with fresh cream and strawberries.

'Decadent,' she commented for the waiter's benefit. 'I'll need to run an extra kilometre and do twenty more sit-ups in the morning to combat the extra kilojoules.'

Even when she'd lived with Sloane, she'd preferred the suburban footpaths and fresh air to the professional gym housed in his apartment.

'I can think of something infinitely more enjoyable by way of exercise.'

'Sex?' Was it the wine that had made her suddenly brave? With ladylike delicacy, she indicated his selection of *crème caramel*. 'You should live a little, walk on the wild side.'

'Wild, Suzanne?' His voice was pure silk with the honeyed intonation he used to great effect in the courtroom.

Knowing she would probably lose didn't prevent her from enjoying a verbal sparring. 'Figuratively speaking.'

'Perhaps you'd care to elaborate?'

Her eyes were wide, luminous, and tinged with wicked humour. 'Do the unexpected.'

Very few women sought to challenge him on any level, and none had in quite the same manner this petite, independent blonde employed. 'Define unexpected.'

Her head tilted to one side. 'Be less—conventional.'

'You think I should play more?' The subtle emphasis was intended, and he watched the slight flicker of her lashes, the faint pink that coloured her cheeks. Glimpsed the way her throat moved as she swallowed. And felt a sense of satisfaction. With innate skill, he honed the blade and pierced her vulnerable heart. 'I have a vivid memory of just how well we *played* together.'

So did she, damn him. Very carefully she replaced her spoon on the plate. 'Perhaps you'd care to tell me what arrangements you've made for Friday morning.'

'I've instructed the pilot we'll be leaving at eight.'

'I'll meet you at the airport.'

'Isn't that carrying independence a little too far?'

'Why should you drive to the North Shore, only to have to double back again?' Suzanne countered.

Something shifted in his eyes, then it was successfully masked. 'It isn't a problem.'

Of course it wasn't. *She* was making a problem out of sheer perversity. 'I'll drive to your apartment and garage my car there for the weekend,' she conceded.

Sloane inclined his head in mocking acquiescence. 'If you insist.'

It was a minor victory, one she had the instinctive feeling wasn't a victory at all.

Sloane ordered coffee, then settled the bill. She didn't linger, and he escorted her to the lobby, instructed the concierge to organise her car, and waited until it was brought to the main entrance.

'Goodnight, Suzanne.'

His features appeared extraordinarily dark in the angled shadows, his tone vaguely cynical. An image of sight and sound that remained with her long after she slid wearily into bed.

CHAPTER TWO

THURSDAY proved to be a fraught day as Suzanne applied for and was granted two days' leave, then she rescheduled appointments and consultations, attended to the most pressing work, delegated the remainder, *and* donated her entire lunch hour to selecting something suitable to wear to Georgia's wedding.

Dedication to duty ensured she stayed back an extra few hours, and she arrived home shortly after eight, hungry and not a little disgruntled at having to eat on the run while she sorted through clothes and packed.

Elegant, casual, and beachwear, she determined as she riffled through her wardrobe, grateful she had sufficient knowledge of the Wilson-Willoughby lifestyle to know she need select the best of her best.

Comfortable baggy shorts and sweat-tops were out. *In* were tailored trousers, smart shirts, silk dresses, tennis gear. And the obligatory swimwear essential in the tropical north's midwinter temperatures.

Some of Trenton Wilson-Willoughby's guests would arrive with large Louis Vuitton travelling cases containing what they considered the minimum essentials for a weekend sojourn.

Suzanne managed to confine all she needed into one cabin bag, which she stored on the floor at the foot of her bed in readiness for last-minute essentials in the morning, then she returned to the kitchen and took a can of Diet Coke from the refrigerator.

She crossed into the lounge, switched on the television and flicked through the channels in the hope of finding something that might hold her interest. A legal drama, a medical ditto, sport, a foreign movie, and something dire relating to the occult. She switched off the set, collected a magazine and sank into a nearby chair to leaf through the pages.

She felt too restless to settle for long, and after ten minutes she tossed the magazine aside, carried the empty can into the kitchen, then undressed and took a shower.

It wasn't late *late*, but she felt tired and edgy, and knew she should go to bed given the early hour she'd need to rise in the morning.

Except when she did she was unable to sleep, and she tossed and turned, then lay staring at the ceiling for an age.

With a low growl of frustration she slid out of bed and padded into the lounge. If she was going to stare at something, she might as well curl up in a chair and stare at the television.

It was there that she woke, with a stiff neck and the television screen fizzing from a closed channel.

Suzanne peered at her watch in the semi-darkness, saw that it was almost dawn, and groaned. There was no point in crawling back to bed for such a short time. Instead she stretched her legs and wandered into the kitchen to make coffee.

Casual elegance denoted her apparel for the day,

and after a quick shower and something to eat she stepped into linen trousers and a matching silk sleeveless top. Make-up was minimal, a little colour to her cheeks, mascara to give emphasis to her eyes, and a touch of rose-pink to her lips. An upswept hairstyle was likely to come adrift, so she left her hair loose.

At seven she added a trendy black jacket, checked the flat, then she fastened her cabin bag, took it downstairs and secured it in the boot. Then she slid in behind the wheel and reversed her car out onto the road.

At this relatively early hour the traffic flowed freely, and she enjoyed a smooth run through the northern suburbs.

The city skyline was visible as she drew close to the harbour bridge, the tall buildings bathed in a faint post-dawn mist that merged with the greyness of a midwinter morning and hinted at rain.

Even the harbour waters appeared dull and grey, and the ferries traversing its depths seemed to move heavily towards their respective berths.

Once clear of the bridge, it took minimum time to reach the attractive eastern suburb of Rose Bay. Sloane's penthouse apartment was housed in a modern structure only metres from the edge of the wide, curving bay.

A number of large, beautiful old homes graced the tree-lined street and Suzanne admired the elegant two- and three-storeyed structures in brick and paint-washed stucco, situated in attractive landscaped grounds, as she turned into the brick-tiled apron adjoining Sloane's apartment building.

He was waiting for her, his tall frame propped against the driver's side of his sleek, top-of-the-range Jaguar. Casual trousers, an open-necked shirt and jacket had replaced his usual three-piece business suit, and he looked the epitome of the wealthy professional.

The trousers, shirt and jacket were beautifully cut, the shoes hand-stitched Italian. He didn't favour male jewellery, and the only accessory he chose to wear was a thin gold watch whose make was undoubtedly exorbitantly expensive. His wardrobe contained a superb collection, yet none had been acquired as a status symbol.

Suzanne shifted the gear lever into neutral, then she slid out from behind the wheel and turned to greet him. 'Good morning. I'm not late, am I?' She knew she wasn't, but she couldn't resist the query.

Independence was a fine thing in a woman, but Suzanne's strict adherence to it was something Sloane found mildly irritating. His eyes were cool as they swept her slim form. Cream tailored trousers, cream top and black jacket emphasised her slender curves, and lent a heightened sense of fragility to her features. Clever make-up had almost dealt with the shadows beneath her eyes. He derived a certain satisfaction from the knowledge. She obviously hadn't slept any better than he had.

'I'll take your car down into the car park,' Sloane indicated as he removed the cabin bag from her grasp and stowed it in the open boot of his car.

Within minutes he'd transferred her vehicle, then

returned to slide in behind the wheel of his own car. The engine fired, and he eased the Jaguar out onto the road.

'The jet will touch down in Brisbane to collect Trenton and Georgia,' Sloane drawled as the car picked up speed.

Suzanne endeavoured not to show her surprise. 'I thought Trenton would travel with us from Sydney.'

'My father has been in Brisbane for the past week.' He paused to spare her a quick glance, then added with perfect timing, 'Ensuring, so he said, that Georgia didn't have the opportunity to get cold feet.'

Georgia had rarely, if ever, dated. There had been no male friends visiting the house, no succession of temporary 'uncles'. Georgia had been a devoted mother first and foremost, and a dedicated dressmaker who worked from the privacy of her own home.

For as long as Suzanne could remember they'd shared a close bond that was based on affectionate friendship. Genuine equals, rather than simply mother and daughter.

At forty-seven, Georgia was an attractive woman with a slim, petite frame, carefully tended blonde hair, blue eyes, and a wonderfully caring nature. She *deserved* happiness with an equally caring partner.

'From Brisbane we'll fly direct to Dunk Island, then take the launch to Bedarra,' said Sloane.

Suzanne turned her head and took in the moving scenery, the houses where everyone inside them was stirring to begin a new day. Mothers cooking breakfast, sleepy-eyed children preparing to wash and dress before eating and taking public transport to school.

The traffic was beginning to build up, and it was almost eight when Sloane took the turn-off to the airport, then bypassed the main terminal and headed for the area where private aircraft were housed. He gained clearance, and drove onto the apron of bitumen.

Suzanne undid her seat belt and reached for the door-handle, only to pause as he leaned towards her.

'You forgot something.'

Her breath caught as Sloane took hold of her left hand and slid her engagement ring onto her finger.

She looked at the sparkling solitaire diamond, then lifted her head to meet his gaze.

'Trenton and Georgia will think it a little strange if you're not wearing it,' he drawled with hateful cynicism.

The charade was about to begin. A slightly hysterical laugh rose and died in her throat. Who was she kidding? 'This is going to be some weekend.'

'Indeed.'

'Sloane—' She paused, hesitant to say the words, but needing quite desperately to set a few ground rules. 'You won't—'

Dammit, his eyes were too dark, too discerning.

'Won't *what*, Suzanne?'

'Overact.'

His expression remained unchanged. 'Define overacting.'

She should have kept her mouth shut. Parrying words with him was a futile battle, for he always won.

'I'd prefer it if you kept any body contact to a minimum.'

His eyes gleamed with latent humour. 'Afraid, Suzanne?'

'Of you? No, of course not.'

His gaze didn't falter, and she felt the breath hitch in her chest. 'Perhaps you should be,' he intimated softly.

A chill settled over the surface of her skin, and she controlled a desire to shiver. She should call this off *now*. Insist on using his mobile phone so she could ring Georgia and explain.

'No,' Sloane said quietly. 'We'll see it through.'

'You read minds?'

'Yours is particularly transparent.'

It irked her unbearably that he was able to determine her thoughts. With anyone else it was possible to present an impenetrable façade. Sloane dispensed with each and every barrier she erected as if it didn't exist.

Suzanne fervently wished it were Monday, and they were making the return trip. Then the weekend would be over.

A sleek Lear jet bearing the W-W insignia stood waiting for them, its baggage hold open. Sloane transferred their bags, then spoke to the pilot before they boarded.

The interior portrayed the ultimate in luxury. Plush carpets, superior fittings—the jet was a wealthy man's expensive possession.

A slim, attractive stewardess greeted them inside

the cabin. 'If you'd each care to be seated and fasten your seat belts, we'll be ready for immediate take-off.' She moved to close the door and secure it, checked her two passengers were comfortable, then she acknowledged internal clearance via intercom with the pilot.

The jet's engines increased their whining pitch, then the sleek silver plane eased off the bitumen apron and cruised a path to the runway.

Within minutes they were in the air, climbing high in a northerly flight pattern that hugged the coastline.

'Juice, tea or coffee?'

Suzanne opted for juice while Sloane settled for coffee, and when it was served the stewardess retreated into the rear section.

'No laptop?' Suzanne queried as Sloane made no attempt to take optimum advantage of the ensuing few hours. 'No documents to peruse?'

He regarded her thoughtfully. 'The laptop and my briefcase are stowed in the baggage compartment. However, I thought I'd take a break,' he revealed with indolent amusement.

'I have no objection if you want to work.'

'Thereby negating the need for conversation, Suzanne?'

She aimed a slow, sweet smile at him. 'How did you guess?'

Sloane's eyes narrowed fractionally. 'We should, don't you think, ensure our stories match on events during the past three weeks?' He leant back in his chair. 'Minor details like movies we might have seen, the theatre, dinner with friends.'

Separate residences, separate lives. Hectic work-filled days, empty lonely nights.

A particularly lacklustre social calendar, Suzanne conceded on reflection, and was unable to prevent a comparison to the halcyon days when she'd shared Sloane's apartment and his life. Then there had been a succession of dinners, parties, and few evenings to-gether alone at home. Long nights of loving, a won-derfully warm male body to curl into, and being awakened each morning by the stroke of his fingers, his lips.

Something clenched deep inside her, and she closed her eyes, then opened them again in an effort to clear the image.

'Suzanne?'

Clarity of mind was essential, and she met his gaze, acknowledged the enigmatic expression, and managed a slight smile. 'Of course.' Her attendance at the cin-ema had been her only social excursion. She named the movie, and provided him with a brief plot line. 'And you? I imagine you maintained a fairly hectic social schedule?'

'Reasonably quiet,' Sloane relayed. 'I declined a dinner invitation with the Parkinsons.' His level gaze held hers. 'You supposedly had a migraine.'

'And the rest of the time?'

His expression held a degree of cynical humour. 'We dined *à deux*, or stayed home.'

Suzanne remembered too well what had inevitably

transpired during the evenings they'd stayed in. The long, slow foreplay that had begun when they'd entered the apartment. Sipping from each other's glass, offering morsels of food as they'd eaten a leisurely meal. A liqueur coffee, and the deliberate choice of viewing cable television or a video. The drift of fingers over sensitised skin, the soft touch of lips savouring delicate hollows, a sensual awakening that had held the promise of continued arousal and the ultimate coupling of two people who had delighted in each other on every plane.

Sometimes there had been no foreplay at all. Just compelling passion, the melding of mouths as urgent fingers had freed buttons and dispensed with clothes. Occasionally they hadn't even made it to the bedroom.

Suzanne met his gaze and held it, fought against a compulsive movement in her throat as she contained the lump lodged there, and chose not to comment.

A hollow laugh died before it was born. Who was she kidding? There was no choice at all. If she opened her mouth, only the most strangled of sounds would emerge.

She saw the darkness reflected in his eyes, glimpsed the flare of passion and his banking of it, then wanted to die as his lips curved into a slow, sensual smile.

'Memories, Suzanne?'

Try for lightness, a touch of humour. Then he'd never know just how much she ached inside. 'Some of them were good, very good.' He deserved that, if nothing else. Others were particularly forgettable. Such as the bitchiness of some of his social equals.

Oh, damn. She was treading into deeper water with every step she took. And she'd only been in his company an hour. What state would she be in at the end of the weekend, for heaven's sake?

She fished a magazine from a strategically placed pocket, and began flipping through the glossy pages until she discovered an article that held her interest. Or at least she could feign that it did for the duration of the short flight to Brisbane.

It was a relief when the jet landed and cruised to a halt on the far side of the terminal. Suzanne glimpsed a limousine parked close to the hangar, and Sloane's father boarded as soon as the jet's door opened and the steps were unfolded.

'Good morning.'

Trenton moved lithely down the aisle and closed the distance to greet them.

The family resemblance between father and son was clearly evident, the frame almost identical, although Trenton was a little heavier through the chest, slightly thicker in the waist, and his hair was streaked with grey.

He was a kind man, possessed of a gentle wit, beneath which was a shrewd and knowledgeable business mind.

Suzanne rose to her feet and allowed herself to be enveloped in a bear-hug.

'Suzanne. Lovely to see you, my dear.' He released her, and acknowledged his son with a warm smile.

'Sloane.' He indicated the limousine. 'Georgia is making a call from the car.' The smile broadened, and his eyes twinkled with humour as he placed a hand on Suzanne's shoulder. 'A last-minute confirmation of floral arrangements for the wedding. Go down and talk to her while I check the luggage being loaded on board.'

Georgia was fixing her lipstick, a slight pink colouring her cheeks as Suzanne slid into the rear seat, and she leaned forward and brushed her mother's cheek with her own. 'Nervous?'

'No,' her mother denied. 'Just needing someone to tell me I'm not being foolish.'

Georgia had been widowed at a young age, left to rear a child who retained little memory of the father who had been killed on a dark road in the depth of night by a joyriding, unlicensed lout high on drugs and alcohol. Life thereafter hadn't exactly been a struggle, as circumspect saving and a relatively strict budget had ensured there were holidays and a few of life's pleasures.

'You're not being foolish,' Suzanne said gently.

Georgia appeared anxious as she lifted a hand and pressed fingers to Suzanne's cheek. 'I would have preferred to put my plans on hold until after your wedding to Sloane. You don't mind, do you?'

It was difficult to maintain her existing expression beneath the degree of guilt and remorse she experienced for embarking on a deliberately deceitful course.

'Don't be silly, Mama,' she said gently. 'Sloane has

briefs stacked back to back. We can't plan anything until he's free to take a few weeks' break.' She tried for levity, and won. 'Besides, I doubt Trenton would hear of any delay.'

'No,' a deep voice drawled. 'He wouldn't.'

Trenton held out his hand and Suzanne took it, then stepped out of the car, watching as he gave Georgia a teasing look. 'Time to fly, sweetheart.'

Suzanne boarded the jet, closely followed by her mother and Trenton, and within minutes the jet cruised a path to a distant runway, paused for clearance, then accelerated for take-off.

An intimate cabin, intimate company, with the emphasis on *intimacy*. It took only one look to see that Trenton was equally enamoured of Georgia as she was of him.

Any doubts Suzanne might have had were soon dispensed with, for there was a magical chemistry existent that tore the breath from her throat.

You shared a similar alchemy with Sloane, an inner voice taunted.

Almost as soon as the 'fasten seat belts' sign flashed off Trenton rose to his feet and extracted a bottle of champagne and four flutes from the bar fridge.

'A toast is fitting, don't you agree?' He removed the cork and proceeded to fill each flute with vintage Dom Perignon, handed them round, then raised his own. 'To health, happiness—' his eyes met and held Georgia's, then he turned to spare Sloane and Suzanne a carefree smile '—and love.'

Sloane touched the rim of his flute to that of Suzanne's, and his gaze held a warmth that almost stole her breath away.

Careful, she cautioned. It's only an act. And, because of it, she was able to direct him a stunning smile before turning towards her mother and Trenton. 'To you both.'

Alcohol before lunch was something she usually chose to avoid, and champagne on a near-empty stomach wasn't the wisest way to proceed with the day.

Thankfully there was a selection of wafer-thin sandwiches set out on a platter, and she ate one before sipping more champagne.

Sloane lifted a hand and tucked a stray tendril of hair back behind her ear in a deliberately evocative gesture. It pleased him to see her eyelashes sweep wide, feel the faint quiver beneath his touch, and glimpse the increased pulse-beat at the base of her throat.

It would prove to be an interesting four days. And three nights, he perceived with a degree of cynical amusement.

Suzanne felt the breath hitch in her throat. *Was she out of her mind?* What had seemed a logical, common-sense option now loomed as an emotional minefield.

CHAPTER THREE

BEDARRA ISLAND resembled a lush green jewel in a sapphire sea. Secluded, reclusive, a haven of natural beauty, and reached only by launch from nearby Dunk Island.

Bedarra Island at first sight appeared covered entirely by rainforest. It wasn't until the launch drew closer that Suzanne glimpsed a high-domed terracotta-tiled villa roof peeping through dense foliage, then another and another.

There were sixteen private villas, walking was the only form of transport, and children under fifteen were not catered for, she mused idly, having studied the brochure she'd collected the day after she'd become aware of their destination.

She stood admiring the translucent sea as the launch cleaved through the water. It looked such a peaceful haven, the ideal place to get away from the rush and bustle of city life.

Acute sensory perception alerted her to Sloane's presence, and she contained a faint shivery sensation as he moved in close behind her, successfully forming a casual cage as he placed a hand at either side of her on the railing.

No part of his body touched hers, but she was intensely aware of the few inches separating them and how easy it would be to lean back into that hard-muscled frame.

She closed her eyes against the painful image of memory of when they had stood together just like this. Looking out over a sleeping city from any one of several floor-to-ceiling windows in his penthouse; in the kitchen, where she'd adored taking the domestic role; the large *en suite*. On any one of many occasions when he'd enfolded her close and nuzzled the sensitive slope of her neck, her nape, the hollow behind each earlobe.

Times when she had exulted in his touch and turned into the circle of his arms to lift her face to his for a kiss that was alternately slow and gentle, or hard and hungry. Inevitably, it had led them to the bedroom and long hours of passion.

Suzanne's fingers tightened on the railing as the launch decreased speed and began to ease in against the small jetty. Was Sloane's memory as vivid as her own? Or was he unmoved, and merely playing an expected role?

Damn. She'd have to get a grip on such wayward emotions, or she'd become a nervous wreck!

'Time to disembark.'

She felt rather than heard him move, and the spell was broken as Georgia's voice intruded, mingling with that of Trenton.

'It's beautiful,' Georgia remarked simply as they trod the path through to the main complex and reception.

'Secluded,' Trenton concurred. 'With guaranteed privacy, and no unwanted intrusion by the media.'

For which he was prepared to pay any price, Suzanne concluded, knowing only too well how difficult it was at times to enjoy a private dinner out without being interrupted by some society photographer bent on capturing a scoop for the tabloid social pages.

Exotic native timbers provided a background for the merging colour and tone of furnishings adorning the reception area.

The reception manager greeted them warmly, processed their check-in with practised speed, indicated their luggage would be taken to their individual villas and placed two keys on the counter.

Suzanne felt as if she'd been hit in the solar plexus by a sledgehammer. *Fool.* Of course she and Sloane were to share a villa. Why on earth not, given they were supposedly still engaged and living together?

'We'll meet in the dining room for lunch.' Trenton collected one key and spared his watch a glance. 'Say—half an hour?'

Together they traversed a curving path and reached Trenton and Georgia's villa first, leaving Sloane and Suzanne to continue to their own.

Suzanne could hear the faint screech of birds high in the trees, and she wondered at their breed, whether they were red-crested parrots with their brilliant blue and green plumage, or perhaps the white cockatoo, or pink-breasted galah.

Sloane unlocked the door and she preceded him

inside, waiting only until he closed the door behind him before turning towards him.

'You knew, didn't you?' she demanded with suppressed anger.

'That we'd share? Yes.' He regarded her steadily. 'You surely didn't imagine we'd have separate accommodation?'

She watched as he moved into the room, and wanted to throw something—preferably at him. 'And, of course, as Trenton has booked out the entire island there are no free villas.'

He turned and directed her a level look. 'That's true. Although even if there were we'd still share.'

'The projected image of togetherness,' Suzanne said with heavy cynicism, and glimpsed one eyebrow slant in silent query.

'Something we agreed as being the favoured option, I believe?'

A temporary moment of insanity when she'd put her mother's feelings to the forefront with very little thought for her own, she decided disparagingly. Then felt bad, for she'd do anything rather than upset Georgia.

The villa was spacious, open-plan living on two levels. And it was remarkably easy to determine via an open staircase that the upper level was given over to one bedroom, albeit that it was large and housed a queen and single bed, as well as an adjoining *en suite* bathroom.

Suzanne followed him upstairs, and discovered the bedroom was larger than she'd expected, with glossy timber floors and a high ceiling. A central fan stirred recycled air-conditioned air, and dense external foliage provided an almost jungle-like atmosphere that heightened the sensation of secluded tranquillity.

Her eyes skimmed over both beds, and quickly skittered towards the functional *en suite*. Four days of enforced sharing. It had hardly begun, and already she could feel several nerve-ends curling in protective self-defence.

'Which bed would you prefer?' she asked in civil tones, wanting, needing to set down a few ground rules. Rules were good, they imposed boundaries, and if they adhered to them they should be able to get through the weekend with minimum conflict.

He regarded her thoughtfully. 'You don't want to share?'

'No.' She didn't want to think about it, didn't *dare*. It was bad enough having to share the same villa, the same bedroom.

To share the same bed was definitely impossible. Unless she was into casual sex, for the sake of sex. And she wasn't. To her, sex meant intimacy, sensuality, *love*. Not a physical exercise to be indulged in simply to satisfy a basic urge.

Sloane watched her expressive features, perceived each deliberation and recognised every one of them. 'Pity.'

Suzanne's lashes swept upwards, and her eyes sparked with anger. 'You surely didn't expect me to agree?'

'No.' His smile held wry humour, and there was a

musing gleam evident in the depth of his appraisal. He reached out an idle finger and touched its tip to the end of her nose. The smile broadened. 'But you rise so beautifully to the bait.'

Of all the... She drew in a deep breath, and expelled it slowly in an effort to defuse the simmering heat of her rage. 'I think,' she vouchsafed with the utmost care, 'we had better agree not to ruffle each other's feathers. Or we're likely to come to blows.'

'Verbal, of course.'

His faint mockery further incensed her. '*Physical*, if you don't watch your step!'

'Now there's an interesting image.' He gave a silent laugh, and his eyes were as dark as she imagined the devil's own to be. 'A word of warning, Suzanne,' he said softly. 'Don't expect me to behave like a gentleman.'

This conversation had veered way off course, and she attempted to get back on it. With deliberate calm she turned her attention to one bed, then the other, entertained a brief image of Sloane attempting to fold his lengthy frame into the single one, and made a decision. 'You can have the larger bed.'

'Generous of you.'

'Half the wardrobe is mine,' she managed firmly. 'With equal time and space in the bathroom.'

A lazy smile curved the edges of his mouth. 'Done.'

She looked at him warily. His calm acceptance of her suggested sleeping arrangement was...unexpected.

There was a loud knock on the door, and Sloane moved indolently downstairs to allow the porter to deposit their bags, then, taking hold of one in each hand, he ascended the short flight of stairs.

'I'll unpack.' A prosaic task that would take only minutes.

She was all too aware of Sloane's matching actions as she hung a few changes of clothes on hangers in the wardrobe, lay underclothes into a drawer, and set out toiletries and make-up on one half of the vanity unit.

'Anything for valet pressing?'

'No.' She watched as he extracted the appropriate bag, added two shirts, then filled in the slip and slung it down onto the bed.

'When you're ready, we'll go join Georgia and Trenton in the dining room.'

She needed to run a quick brush through her hair and retouch her lipstick. 'Give me a few minutes.'

In the *en suite* she regarded her mirror image with critical appraisal. Her eyes were too darkly pensive, her features too pale.

A few swift strokes of eyeshadow, blusher and lipstick added essential colour, and she made a split-second decision to twist the length of her hair into a careless knot atop her head.

Her hand automatically reached for the light *parfum* spray Sloane had gifted her. Her fingers hesitated, then retreated.

Oh, to hell with it. She wore perfume because she liked the fragrance, not because of any attempt to tantalise a man. If Sloane chose to think the fresh application was attributed to *him*, he was mistaken.

A quick spray to the delicate veins crossing each wrist, the valley between each breast. Better, much better, she determined as she emerged into the bedroom.

Sloane regarded her with one swift encompassing glance, then caught up his sunglasses and held out her own before standing to one side to allow her to precede him down onto the lower level.

Suzanne was supremely conscious of the intense maleness emanating from his broad frame as they stepped outside their villa. It was like a magnet, pulling at something deep inside her, heightening emotions to a level she didn't want to acknowledge.

'Hungry?'

The sun's warmth caressed her skin, the slight breeze teasing free a few tendrils of her hair as she offered him a brilliant smile. 'Yes.'

A gleam lit his expressive eyes, and he gave a soft laugh as he caught hold of her hand and lifted it to his lips.

Her stomach curled at the implied intimacy, and she silently damned the way each and every one of her nerve-ends sprang into acutely sensitised life.

She attempted to pull her hand free without success. 'The act is a little premature, don't you think?'

'Not really, given we're in a public place and unsure who can see and hear us.'

The tinge of humour in his voice brought forth a rueful smile. 'You're enjoying this, aren't you?'

One eyebrow slanted upwards. 'It's a rare opportunity for me to gain an upper hand.'

'Don't overdo it, Sloane,' she warned in a low voice, and glimpsed his mocking smile.

'What a vivid imagination you have.'

Much too vivid. That was the problem.

The restaurant was spacious, with tables set wide apart indoors and beneath the covered terrace. It was a peaceful setting overlooking the wide sweep of the bay as it curved out into the ocean, the bush-clad undulations of the island providing a tranquil remoteness.

'Would you prefer to sit indoors or out on the terrace?'

'The terrace,' Suzanne said without hesitation.

Georgia and Trenton had yet to arrive, and she selected a table protected from the sun's warm rays.

She watched as Sloane folded his length into an adjoining seat, and was grateful for the tinted lenses shading her eyes. They provided a barrier that made it a fraction more comfortable to deal with him.

A silent laugh stuck in her throat. Who was she kidding? No one *dealt* with Sloane. That was his prerogative. Control, which some would call manipulative strategy, was a skill he'd honed to an enviable degree in the business arena. In his private life, he added charm and seductive warmth with dangerous effect.

'Mineral water?'

She met his gaze, partly masked by tinted lenses, and offered a slight smile. 'Orange juice.'

The generous curve of his mouth relaxed and humour tugged its edge. 'Preference, Suzanne? Or a determined effort to thwart me?'

'Why would I want to do that, Sloane,' she queried evenly, 'when the next three days are supposed to project peace, harmony and celebration?'

'Why, indeed?'

His tone was pure silk, with the merest hint of caution should she attempt to try his patience too far in this game they'd each agreed to play.

A young waitress crossed to the table to take their order, her smile bright, her expression faintly envious as her eyes lingered fractionally longer than necessary on Sloane's attractive features.

Suzanne felt a slight stab of something she refused to accept as jealousy. Dammit, *why* was her body so attuned to this man, when she'd determinedly dismissed him from her mind?

It was one thing to uphold when she had the distance and protection of a telephone conversation. It was something else entirely when confronted with his presence, for then the barriers she'd erected seemed in danger of disintegrating into a heap at her feet.

Conversation seemed safer than silence. 'Tell me about the case you're currently involved in.'

'Genuine interest, Suzanne?'

His amused drawl touched a raw nerve. 'What would you prefer? A polite dissertation about the weather?'

'You could try for an unexpurgated version of what motivated you to walk out on me.'

Straight for the jugular. She aimed for levity. Anything else was impossible. 'And risk the possibility of having Georgia and Trenton appear in the middle of a heated discussion?'

He sank back in the chair and folded his hands together behind his head. 'My dear Suzanne, I rarely have the need to raise my voice.'

Why should he resort to anger when he could employ a wealth of words with such innate skill, their delivery sliced with the deadliness of an expertly wielded scalpel? Anger had been *her* emotional defence.

'This isn't the time, or the place.'

The waitress's reappearance bearing a tray containing two tall glasses filled with orange juice and chinking ice cubes brought a halt to the conversation, and Suzanne watched as the young girl made a production of placing decorative coasters down onto the table, followed by each individual glass.

'If there's anything else you need, just call.' The smile was pure female and aimed at Sloane before she turned and retreated to the bar.

'Oh, my,' Suzanne said with saccharine sweetness. 'You don't even have to try.'

His smile held wry cynicism. 'I suppose I should be grateful you noticed it was entirely one-sided.'

I notice, she silently assured him. Everything about you. She reached for her glass, lifted it, and took an appreciative sip of the iced liquid. 'She looks—available.'

His eyes narrowed. 'You forget,' he remarked in a

silky drawl. 'I'm with you.' The words alone were simple. His delivery of them was not.

It cost her to lift one eyebrow in a gesture of ill-concealed mockery. 'It's only day one, and already we're into verbal sparring. What will we both be like at the end of day four?'

There was warm humour evident in his smile, and she felt her stomach clench with something she refused to acknowledge as pain.

'Oh, I don't know,' he replied indolently. 'I'm rather looking forward to the progression.' He lifted his glass and touched its rim to her own. 'Here's to us.'

'There is no *us*,' Suzanne declared adamantly.

'Isn't there?'

She shot him a baleful glare. 'Get too close, Sloane, and you'll discover I bite.'

'Be warned I'll retaliate.'

Yes, he'd do that, and ensure that, while he might permit her to win a battle, he had every intention of winning the war.

It was a chilling thought, and one which had her poised for a stinging response.

'Georgia and Trenton have just entered the restaurant,' he warned, and she changed a glare to a slow, sweet smile, glad of the tinted shield shading her eyes as he leaned forward and brushed his fingers against her cheek.

A blatant action if ever there was one, signalling his intention to take advantage of each and every situation during their island sojourn. If he was intent on playing a game, then it shouldn't be uneven, she decided with a touch of vengeance.

With deliberate calm she captured his hand with her own and brought it to her lips, then used her teeth to nip the soft pad of one finger...*hard*.

Triumph, albeit temporary, was very sweet. Despite the faint warning flare that promised retribution.

'Isn't this an idyllic place?' Georgia enthused as she sank into the chair Trenton held out for her.

'Wonderful,' Suzanne agreed lightly. Almost anything was worth it to see her mother so blissfully happy. Even wielding emotional and verbal swords with Sloane.

'I've checked arrangements with the hotel staff,' Trenton disclosed as he settled into the remaining chair.

The waitress appeared at his side, took an order, then retreated to the bar to fill it.

'Everything's under control.'

Why wouldn't it be? Suzanne questioned silently. The Wilson-Willoughby name was sufficient to ensure assistants scrambled over one another in the need to please.

Success wasn't born of those who were faint-hearted, insecure, or inept. And no one in their right mind could accuse Trenton or Sloane of possessing any one of those character flaws.

Power was the keynote, and with it came a certain ruthlessness Suzanne found difficult to condone. A paradox, for it was a quality she could also admire.

'When do the guests arrive?'

'Tomorrow morning. The launch will make an unscheduled run from Dunk Island.'

Lunch comprised a superb seafood starter, followed by freshly caught grilled fish and salad, and they each chose a selection of succulent fresh fruit for dessert.

'Have I met each of the invited guests?' Suzanne voiced the query with what she hoped was casual interest, and tried to ignore the faint knot twisting in her stomach as she waited for Trenton's response.

Sloane's eyes sharpened, although his expression remained unchanged.

'I'm almost certain of it,' Trenton concurred with a relaxed smile. He named them, and Suzanne endeavoured to breathe normally as she waited for one specific name, and felt the easing of tension when it wasn't mentioned.

Sloane was aware of every nuance, every gesture, no matter how slight. His suspicions, laser-sharp, moved up a notch.

'Shall we leave?' Georgia broached with a sunny smile. 'I haven't finished unpacking, and there are a few things I want to check on.'

Sloane rose to his feet, and held Suzanne's chair as she followed his actions. His hand brushed her arm, and she felt warmth flood her veins in an instantaneous reaction to his touch. There was little she could do to prevent the casual arm he placed around her waist as he led her from the restaurant. Nor could she give in to temptation and shrug it off as they lingered outside.

With a hint of desperation she turned towards her

mother. 'Do you need help with anything this afternoon?' Say *yes*. *Please*, she begged silently, doubtful anyone, least of all her radiant mother, would take heed. Murphy's law had prevailed from the moment she'd picked up the phone the day before yesterday to take Georgia's call.

'Oh, darling, thank you. But no, there's nothing.'

Of course not. Anything that needed to be done had been taken care of before Georgia had boarded the plane in Brisbane. And here on this idyllic island there were ample staff to cater to a guest's slightest whim.

'The past few days have been so hectic,' Georgia continued, sparing Trenton a warm glance. 'Now that we're here, I just want to relax.' The warmth heated, and was diffused with a generous, faintly humorous smile. 'You and Sloane take time out to explore. We'll join you for a drink before dinner. Shall we say six?'

There was little to do except agree, and Suzanne suffered Sloane's loose hold as he led the way back to their villa, pulling free as soon as they were safely inside with the door closed behind them.

Suzanne glanced around the elegant tropical-designed furnishings, the four spacious walls, and felt the need to escape.

'I think I'll go for a walk.' She moved towards the stairs leading to the bedroom. She'd change into cotton shorts and sleeveless top, and exchange her shoes for light trainers.

'I'll come with you.'

His drawling tone halted her steps and she turned to face him. 'What if I don't want you to?'

'Tough.'

Anger rose to the surface, tingeing her cheeks with colour, and adding a dangerous sparkle to her eyes. 'You're determined to make this as difficult as possible, aren't you?'

He closed the distance between them. 'Everything we do this weekend, we do together. Understood?'

'*Everything*, Sloane?' Her chin tilted. 'Isn't that a bit too *literal*?'

Those dark eyes above her own hardened fractionally, and she forced herself not to blink as he lifted a hand and cupped her cheek. 'We agreed to a temporary truce. Let's try to keep it, shall we?'

She'd never seen him lose his temper, only witnessed a chilled expression turn his eyes almost black, detected the ice in his voice more than once in the courtroom, and on a few occasions when dealing with an adversary over the phone. But never with her.

A faint shiver shimmied across the surface of her skin, and she fought to diffuse the intense, potentially dangerous air that swirled between them.

'I hope you packed trainers,' she said lightly. 'Those hand-stitched Italian shoes you wear weren't made for trekking through sand and bush.'

The edges of his mouth quirked, then relaxed into a musing smile. 'A temporary escape, Suzanne?'

'Got it in one.'

His thumb brushed across her lower lip, then he let

his hand fall to his side. 'Give me a few minutes to change, then let's go try to enjoy it.'

She ascended the stairs and quickly changed, deciding on the spur of the moment to don a bikini beneath shorts and top. With a deft movement she pulled on a peaked cap, slid her sunglasses into place, caught up a towel and turned to face him.

'Ready?'

Shorts had replaced tailored trousers, and the hand-stitched shoes had been exchanged for trainers. He looked, Suzanne decided, relaxed and at ease. A projected persona that could be infinitely deceiving.

She followed in his wake, aware of the broad set of his shoulders, the powerful back beneath the cotton polo shirt. The exclusive tones of his cologne teased her senses, heightening them to a degree that made her want to scream.

Elusive scents, the movement of honed muscle and sinew, *knowing* their power, the sensual magic this one man could create within her—it was torture.

It had taken her every hour of every day since she'd left him to build up invisible walls from within which she could protect and defend herself against his powerful alchemy. Night after night she'd lain awake rationalising her motives for leaving him; applied logic, indulged in amateur psychology, and resolved that she'd reached a satisfactory and sane decision.

Yet somehow instinct continued to war with rationale, and she disliked the contrariness of her ambivalence.

'OK, where shall we begin?' Determination was the key. 'The beach?'

'Why not?'

Sloane's voice held a tinge of amusement, and she spared him a searching glance for evidence of cynical humour. However, it was impossible to detect anything behind the dark lenses of his sunglasses.

CHAPTER FOUR

THE sand resembled light honey, marked high by a thin line of shells, most broken, some whole, and scraps of seaweed: the flotsam of an outgoing tide.

Suzanne paused every now and then to select a few, only to send them skimming out into the translucent blue-green water.

It was quiet, so quiet as to imagine there was no one else on the island. The sun was pleasantly warm in a tropical climate known as the winterless north, and tempered only by a slight breeze drifting in from the sea.

She was supremely conscious of the man at her side; how, now she was in casual trainers, her height seemed diminished in comparison to his. It made her feel fragile and vaguely vulnerable, which was crazy.

'Do you want to clamber over those rocks and discover what's on the other side?'

They had followed the beach's gentle curve to a wide outcrop of boulders that separated land and sea.

Anything was better than going back to their villa. 'OK.'

They came to a small cove, the shallows bounded by an irregular scatter of huge boulders, and patches of soft crunchy sand above the shoreline. Isolated, and quite breathtakingly beautiful.

'Want to continue on?'

'Swim,' Suzanne said without hesitation, and she spared him a quick glance.

His warm smile caused the breath to catch in her throat. 'I'll join you.'

Was he wearing briefs? This was a sufficiently isolated spot for it not to matter. So why should it bother her? Except it did, of course. Badly.

'You object?' His soft drawl made her stomach dip and execute a series of slow somersaults.

'No, of course not.' How come a decision to swim suddenly seemed dangerous? *Fool*, she silently castigated herself as she quickly stripped down to her bikini.

Suzanne was conscious of Sloane matching her actions, and a surreptitious glance beneath her lashes was sufficient to determine that thin black silk provided an adequate covering.

Although *adequate* hardly equated with a hard-muscled masculine frame at the peak of physical fitness. A visual attestation of powerful male destined to cause the female heart to leap into a quickened beat.

Yet it was more than that, much more.

Sloane possessed a primitive magnetism, an animalistic sense of power which, combined with an intimate knowledge of the human psyche, set him apart from other men. It was evident in his eyes, an essential hardness that alluded to an old soul, one that had seen much, dealt with it and triumphed. Equally, those dark, almost black depths could soften and warm for a woman, give hint to sensual delight, the promise of devastating sexual pleasure.

Remembering just how devastating had kept her awake nights, tossing and turning in an attempt to forget.

In the daylight hours she could convince herself she was fine, really fine.

Now, she was faced with his constant company for three, almost four days. Mistake; big mistake. Seven hours into this farcical misadventure, and she was already a bundle of nerves, almost jumping out of her skin whenever he came within touching distance.

Why, why, *why* had she put herself in such jeopardy?

For Georgia. Dear sweet Georgia, who *deserved* happiness during her wedding celebration unclouded by an edge of anxiety for her only beloved daughter.

It wasn't so much to ask, was it?

'Do you want to swim, or simply gaze at the ocean?'

Sloane's drawling voice snapped Suzanne's introspection, and she summoned a faint smile.

'Race you in.'

She sprinted into the cool blue-green water until it reached waist-level, then she broke into long, strong strokes that took her a few metres out from the shore.

Seconds later a sleek dark head broke the surface beside her, and she regarded him a trifle warily as she trod water.

'You look,' Sloane said softly, 'as if you're waiting for me to pounce.'

She should never play poker, he decided silently. Her eyes were too expressive. He knew every nuance in her voice, could read each movement of that wide, mobile mouth.

'Why would you do that?' Suzanne queried evenly. 'There's not a soul in sight.'

'No need for you to be under any illusion, hmm?'

He moved close, much too close, and his legs curled around hers before she could attempt to put some distance between them. A hand curved round her waist, while the other held fast her nape, and she didn't have a chance to utter a sound before his mouth closed over hers in a kiss that was incredibly gentle in its possessiveness.

She felt as if she was drowning, sinking, and entirely at his mercy as he took her down beneath the water's surface. He held her so close she was aware of the pressure of his body, the strength of his arousal, the absorption of his mouth on hers, then the power of his thighs as he kicked to bring them up for air.

The breath tore at her throat, and she gasped deeply as he released her mouth and slowly eased his hold. Her eyes were wide with a mixture of shocked surprise and anger, and her lips moved soundlessly for an instant before she broke into spluttering speech, only to lapse into an inaudible murmur as he pressed a forefinger over her mouth.

'Just so you're not in any doubt,' Sloane murmured in a husky undertone, and covered her mouth with his own.

This time there was nothing gentle about his possession, and her head whirled as his tongue mated with hers, sweeping deeply and in total control. She whimpered as he took his fill, his jaw powerful in its demanding onslaught until compliance was her only option.

She had no idea how long it lasted, only that it seemed an age before the pressure began to ease. She felt the light brush of his lips as he explored the bruised softness of her mouth before he lifted his head.

His eyes were incredibly dark, almost black as he regarded her pale features, and for one infinitesimal second he experienced a tinge of regret.

She wanted to hit him. Would have, if she thought she could connect and physically *hurt* him. Instead, she resorted to words.

'If you've quite finished playing the masterful macho *male*, I'd like to go ashore and dry out.' Nothing would allow her to admit how *shaken* she felt. Or how ravaged.

His soft laughter almost unleashed her control, and she kicked out at him, then swore when she failed to connect.

'Most unladylike,' Sloane chided with an indolence that set her teeth on edge.

'I don't *feel* ladylike,' she assured him, hating him for tearing her emotions to shreds. Claim-staking. A reminder of how it had been between them; a promise of how it could be again.

Without another word she turned and swam back to shore, uncaring whether he followed her or not.

The sun's rays warmed her body as she emerged onto the sand, and she lifted her hands to squeeze excess water from her hair, then combed her fingers through its length so that it would dry more quickly, before tending to the moisture beading her body with a towel.

She possessed naturally fair skin which she took care to protect with sunscreen, and she applied coverage from the slim tube she'd brought with her.

By the time she finished the Lycra bikini was almost dry, and she pulled on shorts and top, slid her feet into trainers, then made her way towards the rocky outcrop to explore…in solitude.

Breathing space, she qualified, uncaring how Sloane chose to occupy himself. As long as it wasn't with her.

There were pools of water trapped in several natural rock hollows, tiny lizards the length of her finger which scattered out of sight, and the occasional shell of a dead crustacean.

She could hear the faint lap of water against the rocks, and every now and then there came the screeching call from parrots disturbed in their natural habitat.

Suzanne rounded the corner, and paused to admire the long curve of clean golden sand stretching to the northern point of the island. Beautiful, she thought, stepping from one rock to another.

Was it some form of sensory perception that made her pause and glance to her rear? Or simply an elusive connection she shared with the one man from whom she'd sought a temporary escape?

Sloane stood highlighted against the sky as he closed the distance between them, and she turned back, quickening her steps.

Foolishly, for she misjudged, slipped, and cushioned her fall with an outstretched hand.

Nothing, she determined within seconds, was twisted or broken. Tomorrow she might have a bruised hip, but she could bear with it. There wasn't even a graze on either leg, and her ankles were both fine.

'What in sweet *hell* were you thinking of?'

Sloane's anger was palpable as he crouched down beside her, and she directed him a dark look as she aimed for brutal honesty.

'Aiming to get down onto the sand before you caught up with me.'

His hands skimmed her arms, her legs with professional ease. 'Are you hurt?'

Now there was a question. If she said her emotions were, what good would it do?

He caught hold of her hands, examined the fine bones, then extended his attention to each palm.

Blood seeped from a deep graze on the fleshy mound beneath her left thumb, and she regarded it with a degree of fascination, wondering why it should sting quite badly when at the time she hadn't been conscious of it at all.

'I'll go wash it in the sea.'

'It needs antiseptic.'

She gave a slight shrug. 'So I'll put some on when I get back to the villa.'

Sloane gave her a penetrating look. 'Are your tetanus shots up to date?'

'Oh, for heaven's sake. *Yes.*' She tried to wrench her hand from his grasp. Unsuccessfully, which only served to increase her exasperation.

His eyes were steady, their depths too intensely dark for her to mistake the implacability evident, then without a further word he lifted her hand to his lips, took the fleshy mound into his mouth, and began cleansing the wound with his tongue.

The provocative action caused sensation to feather the length of her spine, and she suppressed a faint shiver at the sheer power of her emotions.

Everything faded beyond the periphery of her vision. There was only the man as she became caught up in the spell of him. Acute sensuality, so potent it robbed the strength from her limbs.

She was aware of the soft body hair that curled darkly, visible in the deep V of his polo shirt, and the faint musky aroma of cologne and salt emanating from his skin.

Her heart began to race, and she became supremely conscious of the need to regulate her breathing in an effort to portray a dispassionate calmness.

Fire coursed through her veins, heating pleasure that pooled in each erogenous zone and became evident with every pulsing beat.

This close, it was possible to detect the dark shadow of almost a day's growth of beard he deemed necessary to dispense with night and morning. It was an intensely masculine feature, and one she found attractive.

Dear heaven, she had to get a grip, otherwise she'd never survive the next few days with any semblance of emotional sanity.

'Don't.' The single negation sounded vaguely husky, and she swallowed compulsively as he raised his head.

'Don't—what?' His eyes pierced hers. 'Take care of you?' His voice dropped a tone. '*Love* you?'

It felt as if a fist slammed into her chest at the last two words, and she held her breath in silent pain. 'Sloane—'

'Another *don't*, Suzanne?' His voice was too quiet, too controlled as he released her hand. 'You think ignoring what we share together will make it go away?'

Her eyes were remarkably clear as they met and held his. 'No. But I plan to work on it.'

'Why?'

The silky tone aroused a dormant rage that coloured her fine-textured skin and turned her eyes to pure crystalline sapphire.

'You don't get it, do you?' The heat emanated from the pores of her skin. '*Love*—' she paused, drew in a deep breath, then expelled it '—doesn't provide a security blanket against reality.' She rose to her feet in one fluid movement, and immediately lost the momentary advantage as he followed her actions.

'You demean my intelligence.'

'Really?' Her chin tilted in open contempt. 'Then perhaps you should consider re-evaluating it.'

She turned away and traversed the few remaining rocks to the sandy stretch below, aware that he followed close behind.

'Suzanne.'

She swung round to face him. *Fine*. If a confrontation was what he wanted, then so be it!

'What do you want, Sloane? A pound of my flesh because I dared assess a situation, and decided retreat was the wisest course of action?' She was defiant, determined to hide the utter defencelessness she hadn't been able to deal with then, any more than she could now.

His eyes darkened into a deep flaming brilliance. 'Dammit, were you so emotionally unsure of yourself—of *me*, that you felt the only option you had was to throw in the towel?'

Anger flashed in her clear blue eyes. 'I didn't throw in the towel!'

A slight smile curved his mouth, lending it a cynical edge. 'Yes, you did.'

'No, I didn't!'

One eyebrow rose slightly. 'What would you call it?'

'A tactical withdrawal.'

He was silent for several long minutes, his regard unwavering. 'You possess a high degree of common sense.' His gaze intensified, and his eyes became incredibly dark. 'Sufficient, I would have thought, to judge me for the man I am beneath the superficiality of material possessions.'

It hurt to enunciate the words without allowing a slight catch to affect her voice. 'Oh, I did, Sloane. I fell in love with the man.' Her expression became pensive, her eyes incredibly sad. 'Then I discovered it was impossible to separate the man from everything that comes with the Wilson-Willoughby tag.'

'On that basis, you took the easy route and threw what we had together away?'

She felt like a laboratory specimen being examined beneath a microscope, and at that precise moment she hated him. 'Damn you, Sloane! What was I supposed to do?'

'Stay.'

One word. Yet it conveyed so much. 'I'm not into masochism.'

His eyes narrowed. 'What in hell are you talking about?'

'*You* are regarded as the ultimate prize in a field of wealthy, well-connected men.' A tight smile momentarily widened her mouth. 'And I, heaven forgive me, am merely a nonentity who dared to usurp each and every one of the women aspiring to share your life.'

The hurt, some of the pain clouded her eyes, and her lashes lowered to form a protective veil. 'I chose not to compete.' There was more, much more she could have said. Repeated the bitchy comments, relayed one very real threat.

'Unnecessary, when there was no contest.' Sloane enunciated the words with quiet emphasis, and felt a wrench of pain at the momentary sadness reflected in her expression.

'No?'

'You hold me responsible for other women's aspirations?'

Her hands clenched until the knuckles showed white, although she managed to keep her voice remarkably calm. 'No more than I hold you responsible for being who you are.'

He wanted to shake her. 'And, being *who I am*, I should select any one of several society princesses from the requisite gene pool, have her grace my arm, my bed, and produce the expected two children?'

The image hurt. So much, it was all she could do not to close her eyes in an attempt to shut it out.

'Be content with a marriage devoid of passion?' Sloane persisted ruthlessly. 'Based on duty and a degree of affection?' His voice lowered and became almost brutally merciless. 'Is that what you're saying?'

Her eyes flashed with latent anger at his analytical and persistent questioning. 'Damn you! I'm not on the witness stand.'

He didn't touch her, but she felt as if he had. 'Humour me. Pretend that you are.'

'And play the truth deal, entirely for your benefit? Sorry, Sloane. I'm not in favour of game-playing.'

His eyes held hers, and she was unable to look away. 'Neither am I.'

'Yet you do it every day in the courtroom,' Suzanne retaliated, and saw his mouth form a cynical twist.

'I don't allow my profession to intrude into my personal life.'

His compelling scrutiny was unsettling, and her eyes gleamed with hidden anger. 'You're so skilled with word play, I doubt it's possible to separate one from the other.'

'You think so?' He moved forward, and she had to forcibly refrain from taking a step backwards. His action wasn't intimidating, but nevertheless she felt threatened.

'Sloane—'

He lifted a hand and brushed a thumb along her jawline. 'Tell me the love changed.'

Oh, God. She closed her eyes, then opened them again, stricken by the tearing pain deep inside. She was powerless to move as he lowered his mouth to capture hers in a kiss that made her ache for more.

She physically had to prevent her body from leaning into his as she tried to stem the hunger that activated every nerve-ending. It would be so easy to wind her arms up around his neck and hold on as he took her on an emotional ride, the equal of which she'd never experienced with anyone else. Yet eventually the ride would be over, and she'd be left with only battered pride.

The sensual magic that was his alone tore at the very foundation of her being, tugging her free until she had no concept of anything but the heat of his mouth and the wild, sweet promise of heavy, satiated senses as they merged as one entity, meshing mind and soul.

A hollow groan rose and died in her throat at the need for *more*, much more than this. She wanted to dispense with the restriction of their clothes, to feel the texture of his skin, the flex of muscle beneath her hands, and have his lips, his mouth savour every inch of her body as they urged each other from one sensual plane to another.

What are you doing? The insidious query rose silently to taunt her. For a few long seconds she ignored it, then reality intervened as the magnitude of what she was inciting doused the heat and began cooling the warm blood in her veins.

Sloane sensed the moment it happened and mentally cursed the swing of her emotions. For the space of a few seconds he considered conquering the subtle change, then discarded the urge, aware that she would hold it against him.

Instead, he lightened the depth of emotion. Slowly easing the pressure of his mouth as he withdrew his possession, he allowed his lips to linger against her own as he pressed a number of light kisses over the full, slightly swollen contours.

At the same time his hands soothed her body, sliding gently over her slim curves, subtly massaging her nape, the delicate bones at the base of her scalp, the fine slope of her back, the firm waist.

Then his mouth left hers and trailed down the edge of her neck to savour the faint hollows at the base of her throat.

He wanted to lift her into his arms and take her here, *now*, remove what remained of her clothes, his,

and make love until there could be no vestige of doubt
in her mind as to how he felt.

Except she would equate that with sexual satisfaction. And while it would certainly ease the ache it
wasn't enough while there were doubts to appease.
He wanted her mind, her soul. *Everything*.

Who had poisoned the verbal darts and aimed them
with careful precision, sufficient to undermine her
confidence to such a level that she felt the only option
she had was to leave?

Any one of many, came the cynical knowledge as
he ran a mental gamut of numerous female acquain-
tances capable of sowing the seeds of doubt...and rev-
elling in the byplay.

Sloane trailed his lips to her mouth, pressed a warm
kiss to its edge, then withdrew to within touching distance, his smile tinged with a certain wry humour as
he surveyed her bemused expression.

'There's a path leading off from the beach. Shall
we see if it leads back to the villa?'

He was letting her off the hook...for now. She told
herself she was relieved, and made a valiant effort to
ignore the vague stirrings of disappointment.

'Let's go,' Suzanne declared decisively. 'Maybe we
can fit in a set of tennis before dinner.'

His gaze was far too discerning. 'With the intention
of wearing yourself out?'

How could she say she wanted to collapse into bed,
too tired to do anything but sleep, instead of lying
awake for most of the night cautioning herself not to
toss or turn in case the movement disturbed the man

occupying the large bed a short distance from her own?

'I might even permit you to win,' she said lightly. Some chance. He had the height, the strength, the experience to trounce her off the court!

Sloane's husky chuckle set the nerves in her stomach into action, and he slid on his sunglasses, then extended his hand.

Suzanne hesitated fractionally, then threaded slender fingers through his own.

They crossed to a sandy path that curved through increasingly dense rainforest, and initiated a leisurely pace. Sunlight filtered between wide-branched trees, lowering the warm temperature by several degrees.

There had to be a variety of tropical insects, but none was immediately evident. It was so quiet. Peaceful. Almost idyllic. A wonderful place to get away from it all.

If only... She stopped the traitorous thought right there. Life was crowded with 'if only's and 'what if?'s. And in the weeks since she'd moved out of Sloane's apartment she'd covered a plethora of each.

Silence allowed for too much introspection, and she sought a temporary distraction.

'Word has it you'll win a large settlement in the Allenberg trial.'

Sloane had a reputation for scrupulous research and meticulous attention to detail. He enjoyed pitting his skill in the court arena, and was known to accept difficult and complex cases for the mental challenge rather than his barrister's fee.

'Interesting.'

Now there was an ambiguous statement if ever there was one. Interesting that she'd mentioned the brief? Or interesting that she'd opted to veer away from anything personal by way of conversation?

She looked at him carefully. 'You have doubts?'

The path levelled out and began following the shoreline. Leading, she suspected, in a meandering fashion back to the main complex.

'I never discount the element of surprise.'

Suzanne had the strangest feeling he wasn't referring to the brief. 'I imagine you've covered all the angles.' Impossible that he hadn't.

He spared her a penetrating glance, then lightened it with a faint smile. 'It's to be hoped so.'

There was a sense of isolation in the stillness surrounding them. Possible almost to believe they were the only inhabitants on the island.

It was comforting to know that staff and civilisation lay within a short distance. Trenton and Georgia were also in residence, and tomorrow the guests would arrive.

People, in this resort deliberately designed for solitude, would be a welcome advantage, Suzanne determined. It meant there would be plenty of opportunity to socialise, and less time spent alone with Sloane.

CHAPTER FIVE

THE path was clear, but not well trodden, and Suzanne suspected it was deliberately kept that way by the resort management to provide the ambience of lush rainforest.

Sloane walked at her side, matching his stride to her own. How long would it take them to reach the main complex? Ten minutes? Longer? A lot depended on how the path was structured. The trip would be leisurely, she imagined, if the upward slant and winding curves were anything to go by.

'It probably would have been quicker to go back via the beach,' Suzanne offered, and he projected an indolent smile.

'At least this way we don't have to traverse a collection of boulders and rocks.'

She met his gaze with equanimity. 'They were relatively easy to navigate.'

He tipped his head and allowed his sunglasses to slip fractionally down the slope of his nose. One eyebrow lifted as he regarded her with a degree of quizzical humour. 'Yet you slipped and injured yourself.'

'It's the effect you have on people,' she declared with wicked mockery.

'People?'

'They either covet your company or choose to avoid it.'

'That's a particularly basic observation,' he said lazily. 'Would you care to elaborate?'

Her response was a succinct negative, and a husky chuckle emerged from his throat as she quickened her pace to step ahead of him.

The trees provided excellent shade, and did much to reduce the sun's heat. It was a lovely day, a beautiful island, and given different circumstances she would have considered herself in seventh heaven to be here alone with Sloane.

'Suppose you enlighten me as to precisely which verbal exchange, if not by whom, caused you so much grief?'

She drew in a deep breath and released it slowly. 'You don't give up, do you?'

'No.'

Whatever had made her think that he would? 'There's no point.'

'I beg to differ.'

She was mercilessly vengeful. 'I wasn't born into the social hierarchy.' She held up one hand, fingers extended, ready to provide a graphic example by ticking off each one as she cited the given reasons. 'No private schooling. At least, not at one of the few élite establishments. My mother still *works*, would you believe?' She was on a roll. 'How could someone like me dare to think she could compete with the *crème de la crème* of Sydney's society? For you to have a fling with me was quite acceptable, but marriage? *Never.*'

It was impossible to gauge anything from his expression. Dammit, didn't he care how each criticism had been like a finely honed barb that had speared through her heart? *Why* didn't he say anything?

'Your response was no doubt interesting.'

His drawled amusement set her teeth on edge, and she glared at him balefully when he brushed his knuckles across one cheekbone.

'I took the line of least resistance, smiled sweetly and assured her you kept me because I was incredibly good in bed.'

It was *he* who possessed incredible skill, *she* who became a willing wanton at his slightest touch.

'And the rest of it?'

'What makes you think there's more?'

'I can't imagine you taking notice of a few bitchy remarks.'

Verbal threats hadn't worried her. Written missives were something else entirely.

'I received an anonymous note in the mail.'

His eyes sharpened, and there was a still quality about him she found disquieting. 'What type of note?'

'Plain paper with an assemblage of cut-out letters from various news publications.'

'Pasted together and worded to say?'

'I had two days to get out of your life.' Even now she could recall it so vividly.

'Or?'

'I would be sorry.'

A muscle bunched at the edge of his jaw, and a string of pithy oaths escaped in husky condemnation. 'Why in hell didn't you tell me?'

'Because I didn't take it seriously.'

He barely restrained himself from shaking her. 'Something obviously occurred to persuade you otherwise?'

A few isolated incidents which had at first seemed coincidental. Except for one. And her mistake had been an attempt to deal with it herself.

'Suzanne.' Sloane's voice was too quiet. Ominous.

She suppressed a shiver, and held his gaze. 'I was driving home after work, and someone tried to run me off the road, then demonstrated very graphically that the next time I wouldn't be so fortunate.' She paused, and drew in a deep breath. 'It was followed by a personal confrontation demanding I get out of your life.'

'Why in *hell* didn't you tell me?'

She didn't flinch at the icy viciousness of his tone. 'You were away at the time.'

He was hard-pressed not to shake her within an inch of her life. 'That shouldn't have stopped you.'

Her eyes assumed an angry sparkle. 'And what could you have done?'

'Taken the next flight back.'

Knowing the importance of his London-based client and the seriousness of the case...

'Believe it,' Sloane assured her inflexibly.

'I dealt with it myself.'

'How, precisely?'

'Assuring her a full report would be lodged with

the police and followed by legal action if I ever heard from her again.' Her eyes were dark crystalline sapphire, her features pale. 'Or if another suspicious accident should eventuate.'

And removing herself from his apartment, and to all intents and purposes from his life. Choosing not to confide in him, or seek external help. The silent rage deep within him intensified. Putting him through hell, not to mention herself.

Now, there was only one question.

'Who?' His tone hadn't altered, but she recognised the anger beneath the surface. And his immense effort to control it.

'It's my decision not to name her.'

His eyes held a ruthlessness that was frightening. Merciless, almost brutal with intent. 'It isn't your decision to make.'

He was a formidable force, but she refused to back down. 'Yes, it is.'

'You're aware I can override you? Initiate enquiries, and eventually obtain the answer I need?'

Her gaze didn't falter. 'To what end? What charges can you lay? I wasn't molested, or hurt.' Just very badly shaken by a vindictive woman who should have been seeking professional help for a sick obsession.

'Harassment constitutes a threat that, proven, is punishable by law.' His eyes were so dark they resembled obsidian shards.

'I'm as much aware of that as you are.' Her resolve was determined. 'Her father has a very high profile which would be irreparably damaged should this come out. It's out of my respect for him that I've chosen to keep quiet.'

He held onto control by a bare thread, and wondered if she knew just how close he was to full-blown anger. Twelve inches less in height and half his weight didn't diminish her stance in comparison to his own. Nor did she reflect any fear. Just steadfast intent that would be difficult to bend. But not impossible.

'You disappoint me.'

She was already ahead of him, for she'd had weeks to prepare for this moment. 'A psychological shift into skilled tactician mode, Sloane?' Her chin tilted fractionally. 'Don't waste your time. Or attempt to persuade me that *love conquers all*. We're heavily into reality, not fantasy. That combination is immiscible.'

'You want *reality*, Suzanne?'

His head lowered down to hers, his breath warm as it fanned her lips before his mouth settled over hers in a kiss that tore at the foundations of her being.

In an imitation of the sexual act itself, his tongue teased hers in a mating dance so evocatively persuasive that her bones seemed to liquefy, and she lifted her arms and held on as her body instinctively arched into his.

One arm curved across her back, while a hand tangled in her hair, holding her head fast as he deepened the kiss into something so incredibly erotic she lost track of time and place.

Her skin felt alive, each sensory nerve-ending so acutely attuned to this one man's touch that she groaned out loud as one hand cupped her bottom and he lifted her up against his body so that his mouth could pay homage to the slope of her neck, the soft hollows at the base of her throat, before tracing a path to the delicate curve of her breast.

She was incapable of offering any protest as he pulled up her top and undid the clip fastening of her bikini bra, nor when he pushed the thin Lycra aside and sought one rosy peak, taking it into his mouth and suckling it until she cried out at the wealth of sensation that swept through her body.

It wasn't enough, not nearly enough. And her hands clung to his deeply muscled shoulders, then slid down his chest in a tactile exploration of the dark whorls of hair stretching from one male nipple to the other.

She felt the flex of sinew beneath the pads of her fingers as she slid her hands over his ribcage to the back of his waist, slipped beneath the elasticated band of his shorts, then curved low over tensely muscled buttocks to hold him close.

His arousal was a potent entity, a powerfully male shaft pressing against the softness of her belly.

An anguished moan escaped her lips as his hand slid beneath her shorts and bikini briefs and teased the soft curling hair at the apex of her thighs, and she cried out as he sought and found the damp folds guarding entrance to her feminine core.

A touch was all it took. *His* touch. And she climbed a mental wall as he stroked the highly sensitised folds, sending her mindless with a desire so strong it was almost too much to bear.

Her whole body seemed to throb as acute sensation took possession of every nerve-ending, and the blood pulsed through her veins to a quickened beat as awareness transcended onto a higher plane.

Sloane knew he could take her now, here, and she wouldn't stop him. It would be so easy, the act so primal, so intensely satisfying, it took all his strength not to take the final step that would make it happen.

He felt the damp heat of her climax, exulted in her soft, throaty cries, the warm savagery of her mouth on his as she lost herself to him with stunning completeness.

Slowly, gradually, Suzanne became aware of where she was and with whom. And what had almost transpired.

Warmth coloured her cheeks, and he watched as her eyes darkened, then became shadowed as long lashes swept down to form a protective veil.

She didn't struggle as he allowed her to slip down to her feet, and he saw a lump form and rise in her throat, only to fall as her mouth worked silently in an effort to form a few words.

'Don't,' Sloane cautioned gently, and pressed a forefinger to her lips. 'What we share is more powerful than mere sexual gratification.' His eyes darkened, and became almost black. '*That* is the reality I have no intention of abandoning.' His finger slid to the corner of her mouth, then traced the curve of her jaw.

He smiled, a soft, slightly humorous, warm curve of his mouth that melted every bone in her body. 'Un-

til the day you can look at me and say the love isn't
there any more. Then…' he paused, and depressed her
lower lip with one forefinger '…I might listen to you.'

Suzanne felt as ambivalent as a feather floating in
a fragile breeze. Surely he didn't—couldn't be imply-
ing what she thought he meant?

'Shall we head back?'

Her lips parted, then closed again. 'Sloane, I don't
think—'

'You want to stay here?'

Oh, God, no. She didn't dare. To risk a repeat of
the past—how long? Ten, twenty minutes? A slight
shiver shook her slim shoulders as she remembered
with vivid clarity just how deep her involvement had
been.

Total wipe-out, she accorded silently. If she allowed him to kiss, *touch* her again, she would be reduced to begging for the wildness of total consum-
mation. And that was a divine madness she could ill
afford if she was to walk away from this weekend
with her dignity intact.

Sloane watched the fleeting emotions chase across
her expressive features, and interpreted each and
every one of them.

He extended his hand, and she took it, all too aware
of the way he curled her fingers within the enveloping
warmth of his own.

They followed the path along its winding curve
through the rainforest until it took a steady downward
slant to the beach adjacent to the main complex. Their
conversation was, as if by tacit consent, confined to

inconsequential subjects unrelated to family or anything personal.

It was, Suzanne determined from a quick glance at her watch, almost five. Allowing thirty minutes to shower and wash her hair, then dress for dinner, she had half an hour to spare.

'Want to try out the pool?'

Had he guessed she was hesitant to return to their villa? Determined the reason why?

Tension created knots inside her stomach, and a tiny bubble of faintly hysterical laughter rose in her throat. She was fast becoming an emotional mess. A wicked irony considering she was almost entirely to blame.

It was the *almost* part that bothered her most. Sloane's participation couldn't be ignored, and she could only wonder why. The convenience of casual sex for old times' sake? An attempt to show her what she was missing?

Somehow neither reason seemed to fit the man, and introspection didn't help at all.

Suzanne turned towards Sloane with a brilliant smile. 'Why not?' Suiting words to action, she moved towards the tiled surround area bordering the pool, shrugged off her shirt and shorts, and executed a neat dive.

The water was deliciously cool, and she stroked several lengths with leisurely ease before turning onto her back and allowing her body to float at will.

She could close her eyes and shut out the world. It was so quiet, it was almost possible to believe that everything was right, and here on this idyllic island they were inviolate from the pressures of business and social obligations. No one could get to them, unless they chose to allow it. Paradise, she mused.

A splash sounded loud in the stillness, and seconds later a dark head surfaced a short distance from her own.

'Sleeping in water isn't a good idea,' Sloane drawled, flicking cool, salty droplets onto her midriff.

'I wasn't asleep.'

'First one out gets exclusive use of the shower.' He lifted a hand and trailed idle fingers across her cheek. 'Unless you feel inclined to share?'

Heat suffused her body and pooled deep within, a sensual flaring over which she had no control.

Suzanne caught his dark, gleaming gaze, glimpsed the faint curl of humour tilt the edge of his mouth. Dammit, he was enjoying this.

She offered him a languid smile. 'Do I get a head start?'

His mouth widened and showed his even white teeth. 'I'm feeling generous.'

She jackknifed into racing position. 'First one out, huh?'

She was a strong swimmer, but Sloane had the superior advantage of height and male power. They reached the pool's tiled edge together, and in one synchronised movement levered themselves up onto its perimeter.

'A perfect finish,' Sloane accorded with indolent amusement as he rose to his feet, watching as she smoothed back the streaming length of her hair while matching her movements with his own.

Suzanne bent to collect her clothes. 'Now why doesn't that surprise me?'

'No shared shower, I take it?'

Her fingers stilled at the sudden graphic image, then shook slightly as she thrust first one arm into a sleeve of her shirt, then the other. 'In your dreams, Sloane.'

'That's the problem—they're remarkably vivid.' His voice was silk-soft and dangerous. 'What about yours?'

Glorious Technicolor complete with sound and emotional effects.

Without a further word she turned and stepped quickly towards the path leading to their villa, uncaring whether he followed her or not, grateful that she'd had the foresight to pick up the duplicate key on their way out.

Inside she made straight for the upper level, collected fresh underwear and a silk robe, then entered the *en suite*.

She set the temperature dial to warm, stripped off her clothes, then stepped beneath the cascade of water.

Ten minutes later she emerged into the bedroom, a towel wound turban-fashion around her hair, to discover Sloane in the process of selecting casual trousers and shirt.

'Finished?'

He'd discarded his shirt, if in fact he'd opted to put it on when leaving the pool area, and the cotton-knit shorts moulded firm-muscled buttocks, gave credence to the power of his manhood, and accentuated long, heavily muscled thighs. To say nothing of the exposed breadth of chest and shoulder.

Suzanne dragged her eyes away from him. 'I need to use the hair-drier when you're done.' She crossed to the wardrobe and extracted an elegant trouser suit in deep aqua, added matching heeled sandals, and slowly expelled the breath she'd unconsciously held as she heard the *en suite* door close behind him.

Just when she thought she had a handle on which way he would move and when, he did the opposite. If she was of a suspicious mind, she could almost swear he was being deliberately unpredictable.

Suzanne discarded her robe, stepped into the trouser suit, then slid her feet into the sandals, and reached for her make-up bag, only to realise she'd left it in the bathroom earlier.

Damn. What would be Sloane's reaction if she invaded his privacy? After all, it wouldn't be anything new. They'd shared a lot more than a bathroom in the past. Except then the game had been love and they'd been unable to keep their hands off each other.

Whereas now... Now, it was an entirely different ball game. The rules had shifted, and both players had regrouped.

Almost ten minutes later Sloane emerged, showered and freshly shaven, a towel hitched low on his hips.

One eyebrow rose in silent query as he examined her bare complexion. 'Too shy to share the bathroom with me, Suzanne?'

She wanted to hit him. 'You allowed me sole use.'

His husky laughter brought a soft tinge of colour to her cheeks. 'Only because you'd have fought me tooth and nail if I hadn't.' He reached for briefs, loosened the towel, and stepped into them. Trousers followed, and his eyes met hers as he slid home the zip fastener. 'And there isn't enough time to enjoy the fight.' He reached for his shirt and shrugged into it. 'Or its aftermath. If we're to make dinner.'

Anger flared, deepening her colour to a rosy hue, and her eyes assumed the brilliance of dark sapphire. 'There wouldn't *be* an aftermath,' she vouched with unaccustomed vehemence.

His gaze didn't waver for endless seconds, then he conducted a slow, sweeping appraisal of her body.

Suzanne felt as if he touched her. Her skin tingled beneath his probing assessment, and her pulse leapt to a faster beat she was sure had to be visible at the base of her throat. Even her breath seemed to catch, and she had to make a conscious effort to prevent her chest from heaving in tell-tale evidence of his effect on her.

His eyes when they met hers again were dark, faintly mocking and held vague cynicism. 'No?'

Sloane wondered if she knew just how appealing she looked with her hair all damply tousled, her cheeks flushed with an intriguing mix of temper and desire.

It made him want to tumble her down onto the bed and show her, *prove* that what they had together was good. Too good to allow anything or anyone to come between them.

Except afterwards she wouldn't thank him for it, and only hate herself.

He wanted her. Dear heaven, *how* he wanted her. His body ached, painfully, with need. But he was after the long haul, not a short transitory ride.

Suzanne drew herself up to her full height and glared at him balefully. 'If you think that sharing this villa, this *bedroom*, means I'll agree to sex, then you can go to hell!'

Did she imagine he hadn't been there? Ever since the evening he'd entered his apartment and discovered she had gone.

'Go dry your hair, Suzanne. Then I'll take a look at your hand.'

His voice was deceptively quiet, and didn't fool her in the slightest. What she'd perceived as being a dangerous situation had just moved up a notch or two.

Five minutes with the hair-drier was sufficient, a further five took care of her make-up, then she emerged into the bedroom.

Sloane was waiting, standing at the full-length window, and he turned as she crossed the room.

'I have some antiseptic in my wet-pack.'

'It's fine.' She dismissed his offer, and her breath caught as he reached her side. 'Really. There's no need to play nurse.'

'Humour me.'

'This is ridiculous!' Exasperation was a mild word for describing how she felt at being shepherded back into the bathroom, and having her hand examined and dabbed with anti-bacterial solution.

'There. All done,' Sloane said with satisfaction.

'I could easily have done that myself!' She wanted to *hit* him.

'Don't,' he warned with dangerous softness, reading her mind.

'Or you'll do *what*?' she flung, incensed.

'Take all your fine anger,' he threatened in a voice that was pure silk, 'and ensure you expend it in a way you won't forget.'

Her stomach executed a torturous somersault, and for a few endless seconds she forgot to breathe. 'By displaying masculine strength and sexual superiority?' She managed to keep her voice even. 'I don't find caveman tactics a turn-on.'

His eyes were dark, so impossibly dark she found them unfathomable. 'Make no mistake, Suzanne,' Sloane drawled with hateful cynicism. 'There would be no need for coercion of any kind.'

Tension filled the room, an explosive, dangerous entity just waiting for the trigger to let a certain hell break loose.

With considerable effort she banked down her anger, then she turned towards him and marshalled her voice to an incredibly polite level. 'Shall we leave?'

'Wise, Suzanne,' he taunted silkily.

How long would such wisdom last? she wondered with a sense of desperation. Sooner or later she was going to lose control of her temper. With every hour that passed she could feel the pressure of it building, and she hated him for deliberately stoking the fire.

They walked in silence to the main complex and

joined Georgia and Trenton for a drink in the lounge before entering the restaurant.

Dinner was a casual meal eaten alfresco on the terrace, their choice a selection of varied seafood with delicate accompanying sauces. They enjoyed salads, fresh bread brought daily onto the island, and they settled on fresh fruit from a selection of succulent pineapple, cantaloupe, sweet melon, and strawberries, served with a delightful lemon and lime sorbet, for dessert.

They declined coffee, and lingered over tall glasses containing deliciously cool piña colada.

'We thought we might take a walk along the beach,' Trenton declared. 'Care to join us?'

And play gooseberry? 'I've challenged Sloane to a game of tennis,' Suzanne indicated, casting the source of that challenge a singularly sweet smile. 'Haven't I, darling?'

Sloane reached forward and brushed gentle fingers down the length of her bare arm. And smiled as he glimpsed the way her eyes dilated in damnable reaction. 'Indeed. I'll even grant a handicap in your favour.'

'How...' she hesitated fractionally '...kind.' She touched a hand to his, and summoned a doting look. 'Especially when we both know you could run me off the court.'

He didn't miss an opportunity, and his eyes were openly daring as he lifted her hand to his lips and kissed each finger in turn.

'We need to go change first.'

There was hardly any point in saying she'd changed her mind. 'We should wait half an hour.' Her eyes took on a wicked gleam. 'Exercise so soon after a meal isn't advisable.' Her mouth curved into a winsome smile. 'I don't want you to collapse with a heart attack.'

Trenton laughed, and Georgia's eyes twinkled as she rose to her feet. 'I don't think that's likely, darling. Come for a walk with us. That'll fill in some time.'

'Sloane?' Suzanne deferred to him, sparing him a level glance.

'An excellent suggestion, Georgia.' He stood and together they strolled along the path leading down to the beach.

Suzanne slipped off her sandals and held them in one hand, watching as Sloane followed her actions with his shoes, aware that Georgia and Trenton did the same.

It was a beautiful evening, the sky a deep indigo with a clear moon and a sprinkle of stars. The sort of night for lovers, Suzanne perceived as she stepped onto the sand and felt its firm crunch beneath her feet.

There wasn't much she could do about the hard, masculine arm that curved along the back of her waist as they formed a foursome and began following the gentle curve of the bay.

'Do you have everything ready for tomorrow, Mama?' Suzanne queried, conscious of the man who walked at her side. The arm that bound her to him would tighten if she attempted to put some distance between them. For a moment she almost considered it, simply for the sake of enforcing her position, only to discard it as she thought of the consequences.

'Yes.' Georgia cast her a warm glance in the semi-darkness. 'Although I probably won't sleep tonight as I go through everything again and again in my mind.'

'I have a remedy for that,' Trenton declared, and Georgia laughed.

'Perhaps we'll join you later for a game of tennis. How long do you intend to play?'

'I'll leave it up to Suzanne,' Sloane drawled, and she turned towards him with a sweet smile that was lost in the fading light.

'Passing the buck, darling? What if I'm feeling particularly energetic?' As soon as the words left her mouth she wanted to curse herself for uttering them.

'I think I can match you.'

In more ways than one. Silence, she decided, was golden. Something she intended to observe unless anyone asked her a specific question.

The ocean resembled a dark mass that merged with the sky. There were no visible lights, no silvery path reflected from a low-set moon. Tonight it rose high, a clear milk-white orb in the galaxy.

Suzanne felt the increased pressure of Sloane's fingers at the edge of her waist, and a tiny spiral of sensation unfurled inside her stomach.

'I think we'll turn back,' Sloane declared, drawing to a halt. 'If we don't see you on the court, we'll meet for breakfast. Eight, or earlier?'

'Eight,' Trenton agreed. 'Enjoy.'

As soon as they had progressed out of earshot Suzanne broke free from Sloane's grasp. Lights were visible through the trees, and as they drew close the main complex came into view.

Within minutes they reached their villa, and indoors she quickly changed into shorts and a top, added socks and trainers, aware that Sloane was doing likewise.

Securing the court wasn't a problem, because there were no other guests to compete with. The hiring of racquets and balls was achieved in minutes, and Suzanne preceded Sloane into the enclosure.

CHAPTER SIX

'ONE set, or two?'

'Two,' Suzanne declared as she crossed the court and took up her position at its furthest end.

'A practice rally first,' Sloane called. 'Best of three gets to serve. OK?'

'Sure.'

He had the height, the strength and the expertise to defeat her with minimum effort. It was the measure of the man that he chose not to do so in the following hour as she returned one shot after another, won some, lost most, and while it was an uneven match she managed to finish with two games to her credit in the first set and three in the second. A concession, she was sure, that was as deliberate as it was diplomatic.

'Your backhand has improved.'

Suzanne caught the towel he tossed her, and patted the faint film of sweat from her face and neck. He, damn him, didn't show any visible sign of exertion. Not a drop of sweat, and he was breathing as evenly as if he'd just taken a leisurely walk in the park.

'I expected your serve to singe the ball.'

Sloane's eyes gleamed with latent humour. 'Were you disappointed that it didn't?'

Expending physical energy had been a good idea.

The heat was there, but banked down to a level she could deal with.

'You played as I expected you to,' she responded sweetly, and waited a beat. 'Like a gentleman.'

He rubbed the towel over the back of his neck, and sent her a musing smile. 'Ah, a mark in my favour.'

'Are we keeping score?'

'Believe it.'

Why did she get the instinctive feeling he had his own hidden agenda?

Her agenda was to survive the weekend with her emotions intact. *His* she could only guess at.

'Let's get a drink from the bar, shall we?' Sloane suggested smoothly.

A diversionary tactic which Suzanne let pass only because she was thirsty.

It was an unexpected surprise, and a welcome one, to see Georgia and Trenton seated comfortably at a table adjacent to the well-stocked bar. Surprise, because she'd thought not to see them again before breakfast, and the welcome part was a definite plus, for it meant she wasn't alone with Sloane.

'We thought we'd join you for a game of doubles,' Georgia said as Suzanne slid into a seat at her mother's side.

'Georgia's idea,' Trenton drawled with amused resignation. 'I had another form of exercise in mind.'

'Don't tease, darling. You'll embarrass the children.'

Children? Suzanne looked at Georgia in keen surprise. Those beautiful eyes the colour of her own bore a faintly wicked gleam that promised much to the man seated at her side. Loving sex without artifice, a joyous sharing and caring.

Suzanne felt a lump rise in her throat at the latent emotion evident, and she took a generous sip from the tall glass of iced water a waiter had placed in front of her only moments before.

She risked a glance at Sloane and glimpsed his wry amusement. 'The *children*, of course,' she ventured conversationally, 'are less likely to score a handsome win after expending their energy on court.'

Trenton sent her a devilish smile. 'Georgia and I need any advantage we can get.'

'So sharing a drink is seen as a five-minute break for refreshment?'

'Definitely.'

'Of course, we're playing two sets?'

'One,' Trenton decreed.

'In that case,' Sloane drawled, collecting his racquet as he rose to his feet, 'let's get started.'

Father and son chose not to play competitively, and Georgia and Suzanne were fairly evenly matched. It was a lot of fun. Suzanne couldn't remember ever seeing her mother appear so brilliantly alive, or so happy.

After an hour and a narrow win in Suzanne and Sloane's favour, they exited the floodlit court and crossed to the lounge bar.

Trenton led the way, his arm curved round Georgia's shoulders, and there was little Suzanne could do about the casual arm Sloane placed at her waist.

'A cool drink?' Trenton suggested as they selected a table and sank down into individual chairs. 'Or would you prefer an Irish coffee?'

It was after ten when Trenton and Georgia got to their feet.

'We'll see you at breakfast. Eight o'clock,' Trenton said. He clasped Georgia's hand in his and brought it up to his lips with a warm intimacy. Suzanne felt her heart flip with something she refused to acknowledge as envy.

'Want to follow them, or stay here for a while?'

Suzanne spared Sloane a considering glance from beneath her long-fringed lashes. 'We could take a walk in the moonlight.'

'A delaying tactic, Suzanne?'

Her lashes swept upwards, and she regarded him with ill-concealed mockery. 'How did you guess?'

'Afraid?' His voice was so quiet it sent shivers down her spine.

That was an understatement. But it was fear of herself that made her reluctant to be alone with him. 'Yes.'

'Such simple honesty,' Sloane said with unmistakable indolence. He rose to his feet and extended his hand. It had been a long day. An even longer night lay ahead.

A swift retort rose to her lips, and remained unuttered. 'It's one of my more admirable traits.' She wanted to take hold of his hand, feel it enclose her own, and bask in the warmth of his intimate smile. Yet to do so would amount to a fine madness of a kind she dared not afford.

'One of many.'

She rose, ignored his outstretched hand, and skirted the table *en route* to the entrance. 'Flattery will get you nowhere.'

He drew level with her. 'Try sincerity.'

She spared him a sideways glance, and chose not to comment. She quickened her step, and felt mildly irritated at the ease with which he lengthened his to match it.

They reached their villa, and inside she crossed the lounge and quickly trod the stairs to the bedroom. She paused only long enough to collect her nightshirt before entering the *en suite*, and carefully closed the door behind her.

A foolish, childish action that nevertheless afforded her a measure of satisfaction. Until it was time to emerge some ten minutes later, when all of the former fire had died and wary apprehension reposed in its place.

Sloane was standing at the window, looking out into the darkness.

'Bathroom's all yours.'

He turned to face her, aware of the moment she'd entered the bedroom via the darkened glass reflection.

She looked about sixteen, her skin scrubbed clean, her hair tied back in a pony-tail. Did she have any idea how sexy she looked in that mid-thigh-length tee shirt? As a cover-up the soft cotton merely moulded her firm breasts and was more provocative than designer silk and lace.

'How's the hand?'

Oh, hell, she'd almost forgotten. 'Fine.'

'And your hip?'

Painful, and showing the promise of a nasty bruise. 'OK.' She moved towards the bed she'd nominated as her own, turned back the cover, and slid between the sheets. 'Goodnight.'

'Sweet dreams, Suzanne.'

She didn't care for the mocking humour in his voice, and as soon as the bathroom door closed behind him she propped herself up on one hand and plumped the pillow vigorously with the other, then she shifted onto her left side and almost groaned out loud as her bruised hip came into contact with the mattress.

She was tired, and, if she closed her eyes and willed herself to believe she was comfortable, surely she should sleep.

Suzanne heard the shower run, then stop minutes later. The bathroom door opened, a shaft of light illuminated the room, then there was darkness, the soft pad of Sloane's feet on the polished floorboards as he crossed to the bed, the faint slither of cotton percale, and the almost inaudible depression of mattress springs settling beneath a solid male frame.

Despite counting imaginary sheep and practising various relaxing techniques, Suzanne found sleep remained elusive.

Her hip ached. Throbbed, she corrected, deep into

specific analysis in the darkness of night. Pain-killers would dull the pain's keen edge and help her sleep.

If only she had some. Maybe there was a foil strip in her vanity bag, or, failing that, it was possible Sloane had some in his wet-pack.

Damn, damn, *damn*. If she lay wide awake for much longer, she'd be in a fine state by the end of Georgia and Trenton's wedding festivities.

You would think, she ruefully decided as she slid carefully from the bed, that an over-abundance of emotional and nervous tension together with long walks, rock-clambering, and three sets of tennis, would fell the fittest of the physically fit.

Instead, she felt as if she'd trebled a daily dose of caffeine.

Suzanne crept to the bathroom, closed the door, then switched on the light and rummaged through her vanity bag to no avail. Her fingers delved into Sloane's wet-pack, hesitated, then, driven more by need than courtesy, she separated compartments and almost cried out with relief when she discovered a slim pack of paracetamol.

She broke off two, part-filled a glass with water and swallowed them, then she replaced the glass and switched off the light. She'd allow a few seconds for her eyes to adjust, then she'd open the door and tiptoe back to bed.

It was a remarkably simple plan. Except in attempting to give Sloane's bed a wide berth she veered too far and brushed against a chair.

A soft curse fell from her lips at the same time Sloane activated the bed-lamp.

'What in sweet hell are you doing?'

Suzanne threw him a dark glance, and resorted to flippancy. 'Rearranging the furniture.'

He slid into a sitting position and leaned against the headboard. His dark hair was slightly tousled and he was bare to the waist.

Probably bare beneath the waist as well, she reflected a trifle ruefully, all too aware of his penchant for sleeping nude.

It was too much. *He* was too much.

'You should have turned on the light.'

Oh, sure. The last thing she'd wanted to do was to wake him. Coping with a darkly brooding male wasn't a favoured option.

Suzanne pushed in the chair and took the few steps necessary to reach her bed, then slid carefully between the sheets.

'Headache?'

She should have known he wouldn't leave it alone. The look she cast him held such fulsome anger it was a wonder he didn't *burn*. *'Yes.'* In this instance she had no compunction in resorting to fabrication.

'Want me to give you a neck and scalp massage?'

Oh, God. 'No.' Would he detect the faint desperation in her voice? She hoped not. 'Thank you.'

'Seduction isn't part of the deal,' he drawled with musing cynicism, and she closed her eyes, then opened them again.

He read her far too easily, and it rankled unbearably. 'Well, now, that's a relief,' she said with pseudo-sweetness.

'Unless you want it to be,' Sloane added with killing softness.

The thought of that hard male body curved over her own in a tasting, teasing supplication of each and every pleasure spot filled her with such intense longing it was all she could do to respond, let alone keep her voice even.

'If you come anywhere near me,' she warned in a tense whisper, 'I'll render you serious bodily harm.'

His husky chuckle further enraged her. 'It might almost be worth it.'

Without thought Suzanne picked up the spare pillow and threw it at him, watching in seemingly slow motion as he fielded it and unhurriedly tossed the bedcovers aside.

'Dammit—don't.' She turned and scrambled to the furthest side of the bed, only to give a sharp cry as her hip dragged painfully against the mattress.

It was no contest. She simply didn't have a chance as Sloane's hands caught hold of her shoulders and turned her back to face him.

For a long moment she gazed at him in open defiance, aware that the slightest move, the faintest word would invite crushing retribution.

His eyes were impossibly dark, their depths unfathomable as he reached for the edge of the bedcovers and wrenched them off with one powerful pull of his hand, then drew her down onto the mattress.

His head lowered and she felt one hand grasp hold of her thigh, then slide to her hip.

Her gasp of pain was very real, and he paused, his mouth only inches from her own. She saw his eyes narrow, glimpsed the tiny lines fanning out from each outer edge, and felt him tense for a few long seconds before he slid the hem of her nightshirt to her waist.

It was a long bruise, red, purpling, and growing more ugly with every hour.

He swore, words she'd never heard him use before, and she flinched as he traced the line of her hip-bone, then probed the surrounding flesh.

'You walked through the rainforest,' Sloane said with deadly softness, 'played three sets of tennis, nursing *this*?'

'It didn't hurt much then.'

His eyes appeared as dark obsidian shards, infinitely forbidding. 'It does now.' He levered himself off the bed and descended the stairs to the lower floor.

She heard the chink of glass, the bar-fridge door close, then he was back with a chilled half-bottle in his hand.

'What are you doing?'

'Applying the equivalent of an ice-pack.'

'A magnum of champagne?' Suzanne queried in disbelief, and shivered as the cold frosted glass touched her skin.

'It'll serve the purpose. Now, lie still.'

She didn't plan on moving. Besides, fighting him would prove a futile exercise.

'What did you find to take in the bathroom?'

'Paracetamol,' she said huskily as he adjusted the bottle. 'Two. In your wet-pack,' she added. An icy numbness settled in, minimising the pain, and she closed her eyes so she didn't have to look at him.

The proximity of his male body was a heady entity, despite the skimpy black silk briefs providing a modicum of decency. As a concession to her?

She could smell the clean scent of expensive soap and male deodorant on skin only inches away from her own. All her senses were acutely attuned, almost in recognition of a rare and special alchemy existent in two separate halves that were meant to make a perfect whole.

It didn't make sense. Nothing made sense.

The pain slowly ebbed, and her eyelids grew heavy. Gentle fingers soothed, kneaded, and dispensed with the tight knots in the muscles of her shoulders, back and thighs.

Heaven, she acknowledged as she relaxed and let him work his magic. She made only a token protest when he lifted her into his arms and transferred her to the other bed.

His bed. Her eyes sprang open, and she made to scramble to the edge as he climbed in beside her.

'I don't think this is a good idea,' she said helplessly as he curved an arm beneath her shoulders and drew her close.

'Just shut up and let it be.' He pillowed her head against his chest, then curled an arm round her waist.

He was deliciously warm, and she cautiously moved one arm so that it rested across his midriff.

It was like coming home. *Déjà vu*, she reflected. With one exception. Lacking was the satiation of lovemaking.

The temptation to begin a tactile exploration was strong. Just the slight movement of her fingers and she could trace the outline of his ribcage, tease one brown nipple, then trail a path to his navel.

He possessed a strong-boned frame, with symmetrical muscle structure, textured skin that emanated its own musky male aroma. Clean and slick with sweat at the height of sexual possession, it became an aphrodisiac that drove her wild. Sensual heat, raw and primal. As primitive as the man himself.

Don't even think about it, an inner voice cautioned. Unless you want to dice with dynamite.

Soon he'd fall asleep, then she'd gradually ease free and slip into her own bed.

It was the last coherent thought she had, and she woke to find warm sunshine filtering through the curtains, the smell of fresh coffee teasing her nostrils. One quick glance was all it took to determine she was alone in the bed. Another to see Sloane's broad back curved over a newspaper spread out on the buffet bar.

At that precise moment he turned towards her, almost as if he was acutely attuned to her every move, and his warm smile melted her bones.

'Good morning.'

Suzanne felt awkward, sleep-rumpled, and she dragged a hand over her tousled hair. 'Hi.'

He had the advantage, dressed and freshly shaven,

and she watched him step from the stool and cross to the edge of the bed. 'How is the bruise?'

She caught hold of the sheet in a compulsive movement, almost as if she expected him to insist on a personal inspection. She flexed her leg. 'It doesn't seem to hurt as much.'

'Want to try another makeshift ice-pack?'

In the clear light of day, she didn't want to be beholden to him in any way. *Too late.* You slept with him, remember? *Sleep* being the operative word...but how much more *beholden* could you get?

'I doubt it's necessary,' Suzanne said quickly. Thinking on her feet seemed a vast improvement to staying in bed, and she managed it in one dignified movement. *Dignity* was the key, she assured herself, and being dressed would be better than wandering around in an over-large tee shirt.

She collected underwear, tailored cream linen trousers and a light cotton top *en route* to the *en suite*, emerging ten minutes later feeling refreshed after a quick shower. And in control. Well, she corrected wryly, as much in control as she could hope for in the circumstances!

Sloane checked his watch. 'It's almost eight. If you're ready, we'll go down to the restaurant.'

Lipstick was all it would take, and perhaps a light touch of blusher. 'Give me a minute.'

Georgia and Trenton were already seated beneath the large airy veranda when Suzanne and Sloane arrived.

'We went for a walk along the beach. It was so

quiet and peaceful. Heaven,' Georgia enthused warmly.

Suzanne caught the sparkle in her mother's eyes, glimpsed the soft curve of her mouth as she smiled, and deduced that while the island possessed a magic all its own, *heaven* to Georgia was the man at her side.

'No pre-wedding nerves?' she queried teasingly as she accepted the waitress's offer to fill her cup with coffee.

'A few,' her mother conceded. 'Last-minute doubts about what I've chosen to wear for the ceremony. Whether my heels are too high, and hoping I'll remember to tread carefully so as not to trip. And whether I should wear the hat the salesgirl insisted was just perfect.' Her mouth shook slightly, then widened into a helpless smile. 'I can't decide whether to wear a bright lipstick or go for something pale.'

Suzanne looked at Trenton and grinned. 'Ah, serious stuff, huh?'

He spread his hands wide and responded with an easy smile. 'My assurance that I don't give a damn what she wears doesn't appear to hold much weight.'

'The mysterious vagaries of the female mind,' Sloane remarked, and met Suzanne's mocking glare with gleaming humour.

'Men,' Suzanne denounced him, 'simply have no idea.' She shot her mother a stunning smile. 'After we finish here, I'll come and give you my considered opinion, shall I?'

'Oh, darling. Please. I'd be so grateful.'

'You can safely say goodbye to a few hours,' Sloane inferred aloud to his father, and Suzanne couldn't suppress the bubble of laughter that emerged from her throat.

'At least.' And was totally unprepared for the brush of his fingers across one cheek, and the warm intimacy of his smile.

'Then I suggest we go eat, so you can get started.'

Why, when she lapsed into a comfort zone, did he do something to jolt her out of it? Her eyes clouded. It's an act, just an act. For Georgia and Trenton's benefit.

The breakfast smorgasbord was a delight, comprising several varieties of cereal, fresh fruit, yoghurt, as well as croissants and toast. Sausages, steak, eggs, hashbrowns, mushrooms. A veritable feast.

It was almost nine when they emerged into the sunshine, and the two men opted to retire to the lounge on the pretext of discussing business, while Suzanne and Georgia made their way to the villa Georgia shared with Trenton.

The design was identical to that of their own villa, although the soft furnishings were different, Suzanne noticed as they entered the air-conditioned interior.

Georgia crossed the lounge. 'Come upstairs, darling.'

Suzanne followed and stood to one side as her mother opened the wardrobe, the drawers, and reverently draped each item of apparel over the bed.

'Let's do the fashion parade thing,' Suzanne suggested, shaking her head as Georgia wrinkled her nose. 'It's the only way I can get the complete picture.'

Fifteen minutes later Suzanne stood back and expressed her admiration. 'Perfect. Everything.'

'Even the hat?'

'Especially the hat,' she assured her mother. 'It's stunning.'

Georgia's eyes moistened with gratitude. 'Do you really think so?'

'Really.'

Suzanne stood still, her head tilted to one side as she regarded the slim, beautiful woman in front of her. 'Now, let's take off the hat, get rid of the shoes, and we'll try each lipstick and decide which one suits best.'

The deep rose, definitely. Pale was too pale, and the coral too bright.

'OK,' Suzanne declared as Georgia carefully divested herself of her wedding suit, and hung it back on padded hangers beneath its protective bag. 'All done.' She grinned, and caught hold of her mother's hands. 'You're going to knock 'em dead.'

A warm smile tugged the edges of Georgia's mouth. 'How nice of you to say so, darling.' She drew a deep breath. 'Now, shall we have a cold drink, and talk girl-talk?' A light laugh spilled out, and her eyes danced. 'Isn't that what the prospective bride and her maid of honour are supposed to do?'

Suzanne fetched a bottle of mineral water from the bar-fridge, poured the contents into two glasses and handed one to her mother.

'Here's to health and happiness. A wonderful day. A wonderful life,' she added gently.

Georgia touched the rim of Suzanne's glass in silent acknowledgement. 'You, too, sweetheart.'

They each took an appreciative sip. 'It'll be nice that we'll be living in the same city,' Georgia said a trifle wistfully. 'I can meet you for lunch. We'll attend a lot of the same functions, too, I imagine. And we'll be able to shop together.'

An arrow of pain pierced Suzanne's stomach. The lunch and the shopping part were fine, but attending the same social functions wouldn't be a good idea. In all probability Sloane would be there, and she would rather die than have to watch him with another woman at his side.

'Tell me where you're staying in Paris.' The honeymoon was a safe topic. 'The shops there are supposed to be marvellous. The Eiffel Tower,' she enthused. 'Make sure you take plenty of photos, and write up a diary. I want to hear everything.'

Georgia laughed. 'Not quite everything, darling.'

Suzanne's eyes danced with impish humour. 'Well, no, I guess not.'

Her mother possessed a rare integrity. And charm. Something that came from the heart. Trenton Wilson-Willoughby was a very fortunate man. But then, she guessed he knew that. It explained why he wanted his ring on Georgia's finger without delay.

'Do you remember when we lived in St Lucia in Brisbane?' Georgia reminisced. 'That adorable little terrace house?'

'And the cat who called both adjoining houses *home*?' Suzanne queried, laughing. 'We fed him mince for breakfast, the man next door gave him fresh fish for lunch, and dear old Mrs Simmons dished out tinned salmon for his tea. He was such a gorgeous bundle of grey fluff.'

The school years, carefree for the most part, with increasing study as she decided on the legal fraternity as her profession. University, law school. Dating. Friends.

Hers had been a happy childhood, despite the lack of a father-figure, and there were many memories to cherish. She and Georgia were so close, *friends* and equals rather than mother and daughter. They had shared so much.

And now it was going to change. Don't go down that path, Suzanne mentally chided herself. Today was meant to be happy, joyous.

CHAPTER SEVEN

THE launch deposited the wedding guests, together with the photographer and celebrant, each of whom had undergone a security check at Dunk Island before boarding the chartered launch to ensure no unwanted media were able to intrude.

Suzanne could only admire Trenton's determination that their weekend sojourn, and particularly the wedding itself, remain a strictly private affair.

There would be time for the guests to check into their respective villas, enjoy a leisurely lunch, and explore Bedarra's facilities before assembling next to the main complex for an outdoor marriage ceremony.

Trenton and Sloane joined the guests in the restaurant for lunch, while Georgia and Suzanne ate a light salad together in Georgia's villa.

It ensured there was plenty of time for them to style their hair, complete their make-up, then dress.

Georgia was ready ahead of time, looking lovely, if slightly nervous. Suzanne gave her mother's hand a reassuring squeeze, then quickly stepped into the elegant pale blue silk slip-dress she'd chosen to wear.

There was a matching jacket and shoes, and she opted to leave her hair loose. Make-up was kept to a minimum, except for skilful application of eyeshadow

112

and mascara, and she selected a clear rose lipstick to add colour.

Then she spared her watch a quick glance. 'This is it.' She cast her mother an impish grin. 'Are you OK?' There was no need to ask if there were any last-minute doubts.

Georgia smiled a trifle shakily. 'In half an hour, I'll be fine.'

Suzanne crossed to tuck a hand beneath her mother's elbow. 'Then let's get this show on the road, shall we?'

The short walk to the main complex was achieved in minutes. Georgia didn't falter as she crossed the lawn to where Sloane stood waiting at the head of a stretch of red carpet dividing three small rows of seated guests and leading to an artistically decorated archway, where Trenton waited with the celebrant.

Suzanne felt her breath catch as Sloane turned to-wards her with a slow, warm smile, then he took Georgia's hand in his and walked her down the car-peted aisle.

Suzanne followed, and when they reached the arch-way she moved to Sloane's side as Trenton took hold of Georgia's hand.

Glorious sunshine, the merest hint of a soft breeze, and a small gathering of immediate family and close friends assembled on an idyllic island resort. What more could a bride ask for?

Nothing, if Georgia's radiant expression was any-thing to go by, Suzanne decided, unable to still a faint stirring of wistful envy.

Her mother looked beautiful, and much younger than her forty-seven years as she stood at Trenton's side while the celebrant intoned the words of the marriage ceremony.

Georgia's response was clear, Trenton's deep and meaningful, and his incredibly gentle kiss at the close of the ceremony tugged Suzanne's heartstrings.

She moved forward to congratulate and hug them both, and the faint shimmer of tears in Georgia's eyes was reflected in her own.

Sloane did the unexpected and kissed Suzanne briefly, but hard, and the pressure of his mouth on hers sent her lashes sweeping wide in silent disapproval.

His answering smile didn't come close in explanation, and she stood at his side, almost *anchored* there as they greeted guests, made social small talk, and accepted the occasional gushing compliment about the happiness of the bride and groom.

The encroaching dusk meant everyone moved indoors, and it was essentially *smile* time. In fact, Suzanne smiled so much and so often, her facial muscles began to ache from sheer effort.

'You're doing well,' Sloane drawled as she took a further sip from her flute of champagne.

'Why, thank you, darling. *Wonderfully* well is what I'm aiming for.'

'And a hair's breadth from overkill.'

She cast him a stunning glance. 'No more than anyone else. Even as we speak, deals are being implemented by two of the country's top business moguls.'

Her eyes sparkled wickedly. 'Their respective second wives are at daggers drawn beneath the sophisticated façade as they size up *who* is wearing the more expensive designer outfit.'

'Second and third wife,' Sloane corrected, and she inclined her head in mocking acceptance.

'Sandrine Lanier and Bettina—?' She arched her eyebrows speculatively. 'Just *who* in Sydney's social élite tied the knot with Bettina?'

He lowered his head and brushed his lips against her temple. 'Cynicism doesn't suit you.'

'Ah, but given the right context it can be fun,' she declared solemnly.

'Sandrine works very hard at being the successful wife.'

It was true. The former actress was delightful, and devoted herself tirelessly to charitable causes. She was also an excellent hostess who enjoyed entertaining her husband's business associates. Michel Lanier was a very fortunate man.

Bettina, however, fell into an entirely different category. The glamorous blonde had frequented every social event Suzanne had attended with Sloane. And had taken great pleasure in flirting with him outrageously at every opportunity. As well as with every wealthy eligible man on the social circuit in a bid to cover her options.

'Just who did Bettina choose?' There could be no doubt on that issue!

'Frank Kahler. They married two weeks ago.'

She didn't need to ask. 'You attended the wedding.'

'Yes.' Sloane's acquiescence held a certain wryness for the occasion that had been far too over the top to be described as being in good taste.

What excuse had he given for her absence?

'You were visiting your mother in Brisbane for the weekend.'

Suzanne looked at him, and glimpsed the fine lines fanning out from the corners of his eyes, then her gaze travelled to the vertical crease slashing each cheek, the wide, sensual mouth, and the strong set of his jaw.

'Feasible, in the circumstances, wouldn't you say?'

Very feasible, she silently agreed. 'You could easily have admitted our relationship was over.'

'Now why would I do that?'

'Because it was. *Is*.'

'No.'

'What do you mean, *no*?'

He leaned forward and brushed his lips against her own, and then he raised his head fractionally. His eyes were dark, and appeared so incredibly deep she became momentarily lost.

Her heart thudded in her chest, and for a split second she forgot to breathe. Then reality kicked in, and she took in a deep, ragged breath, then shakily released it.

'Did you honestly think I'd let it rest on the basis of the explanation you presented to me?' Sloane queried, and saw her eyes dilate with something akin to apprehension, then be replaced with an attempt at humour.

'Impossible, of course, that I might have had a

hissy fit about the number of women who fawn over you, and acted on impulse?'

His lips parted to show even white teeth behind an amused smile. 'A hissy fit?' The edge of his mouth curved. 'Now that's an expression which conjures up an interesting image.'

'Doesn't it just?'

His eyes became even darker, and something moved deep within. Something she dared not define. 'Not your style, Suzanne.'

No, it wasn't. Nor did she act on impulse.

'Nor was your note,' Sloane continued in a dangerously mild voice.

'You *know* why I left,' she said fiercely.

'*Whatever* the motivation, the action was all wrong.'

'Sloane. Suzanne. We need you for photographs.' Trenton's voice intruded, and Suzanne drew a deep breath and collected her scattered thoughts as they moved across the room to the position the photographer indicated.

The man was a hired professional, and aware of the scoop his work would create. He wanted the best shots.

It took a while. The eye of the camera was very perceptive, and Suzanne should, she felt, have earned an award for her performance in playing the loving fiancée of the bride's stepson. Not to mention the groom's son.

Afterwards trays of exquisitely presented hors d'oeuvre were proffered and the champagne flowed like water. Background music from a selection of CDs filtered from strategically placed speakers as the guests mixed and mingled.

'Sloane, so *nice* to see you again.'

Suzanne turned at the sound of a breathy feminine voice, and summoned a stunning smile for the second—no, *third* wife of one of Trenton's friends.

'Bettina,' Sloane acknowledged her. 'You've met Suzanne?'

Bettina's laugh was the closest thing to a tinkling bell that Suzanne had ever heard. 'Of course, darling.'

Kittenish, Suzanne decided. Definitely cultivated kitten. The short, tight shell-pink skirt, the almost-too-tight matching camisole top covered by a designer jacket one size too small. Her hair and make-up were perfection, her lacquered nails a work of art, and the jewellery she wore just had to be worth a small fortune. Bored, and with an inclination to flirt.

'Such a cute idea to have an island wedding.' She touched careless fingers to Sloane's sleeve and deliberately fluttered her lashes. 'You will save a dance for me, won't you?' The *moue* was contrived. 'Frank isn't the partying type.'

Frank Kahler was a substantial catch, Suzanne mused, and felt a pang of sympathy for the much older entrepreneur whose fame and fortune were Bettina's main attraction.

'I doubt Suzanne would be willing to share,' Sloane responded with a musing smile.

'Oh, *darling*, of course you must dance with Bettina,' she said in mild reproach, and her eyes shimmered with simmering sensuality. 'After all, I'm the one who gets to take you home.'

He caught hold of her hand and lifted it to his lips, then kissed each finger in turn. 'Indeed,' he intoned softly.

Oh, my, he was good. She could almost believe he meant it. Then she came to her senses, and she smiled, aware that *her* acting ability was on a par with his own.

'I think I'll have some more champagne.' Bettina cast Sloane an arch look from beneath artificially curled lashes. 'You'll fetch another for me, won't you?'

Interesting, Suzanne decided, that Bettina should use such a well-used ploy. Sloane's eyes gleamed in silent recognition, and Suzanne derived a certain pleasure from handing him her flute. 'I think I'll join Bettina. Thank you, *darling*.' The emphasis was very slight, but there nonetheless.

'He's a hunk, isn't he?' Bettina sighed as Sloane turned and began threading his way to the bar.

And then some. 'Yes,' Suzanne agreed, waiting for the moment Bettina would slip in the knife.

'Sloane came alone to my wedding. Were you sick, or something, darling?' A dimple appeared in one cheek, although there was no humour apparent in Bettina's expression. 'For a moment there, I thought you were no longer an item.'

Suzanne hated fabrication, but she refused to give Bettina any satisfaction by differing her story from the one Sloane had provided. 'I was in Brisbane visiting Georgia.'

'Quite a coup.' The almost-green eyes hardened and her expression became brittle. 'Mother and daughter snaring both father and son.'

'Yes, isn't it?' Suzanne's smile was in place, and she appeared perfectly at ease.

'You must have worked very hard.'

'Impossible, of course,' Suzanne said with the utmost charm, 'that Trenton and Georgia could have fallen genuinely in love?'

'Oh, really, Suzanne. No one falls *in love* with a wealthy man. Steering them into marriage involves an extremely delicate strategy.'

'Of the manipulative kind?' There were no rules in this game, and, as loath as she was to play it, she was damned if she'd allow Bettina a victory. 'Is that how you snared Frank?'

'I cater to his needs.'

Suzanne deserved an award for her performance as she touched a finger to the diamond-encrusted watch fastened on Bettina's wrist. 'Catering obviously pays well. Perhaps I should try it.'

'What,' a familiar deep voice drawled, 'should you try?'

Suzanne turned slightly and met Sloane's indolent gaze. She accepted a flute of champagne and watched as he handed another to Bettina.

'Bettina and I were discussing catering to our men's needs.' Her eyes sparkled with deliberate guile. 'My car has been playing up lately, darling. I rather fancy a Porsche Carrera. Black.' Her mouth widened into a beautiful pout as she lifted a finger to her lips, licked it suggestively, then placed it against the centre of his lower lip. 'Perhaps we could negotiate—later?'

Sensation spiralled from her central core as he nipped her finger, then drew it into his mouth and swirled the tip with his tongue before releasing it.

His eyes were dark, gleaming depths reflecting desire and thinly disguised passion. 'I'm sure we can reach an agreeable compromise.'

Are you mad? a tiny voice taunted. Don't you know you're playing with *fire*?

'One imagines you intend tying the knot *soon*?'

'Trenton and Georgia's arrangements have taken precedence over our own,' Sloane informed Bettina smoothly, and incurred her tinkling laugh.

'Don't wait *too* long, darling. There's quite a few who would be happy to push Suzanne out of the way.'

Suzanne saw Sloane's eyes narrow slightly, sensed the predatory stillness, and felt all her muscles tense.

'Should that happen, they'd have me to deal with.' His voice was ominously soft, and intensely dangerous.

Bettina's light laugh held a slight note of incredulity. '*Figuratively* speaking. Not literally, for heaven's sake.'

Sloane's expression didn't change. 'I'm relieved to hear it.' His eyes hardened measurably. 'Any threat, impulsive or premeditated, is something I'd take very seriously.'

His meaning was unmistakable, and Bettina blinked rather rapidly.

'Well, of *course*.' She sipped her champagne, then offered a brilliant smile. 'If you'll excuse me, I really should get back to Frank.'

'Wasn't that just a bit too menacing?'

His eyes were still hard when they swept over Suzanne's features. 'No.'

She opened her mouth, only to have it pressed closed by his in a brief, hard kiss.

'Don't argue.'

Mixing and mingling was a social art form, and Sloane did it extremely well, slowly circulating between guests as he enquired about various family members, listened to an amusing anecdote or two, and shared a few reminiscences.

Dinner was served at seven. Tables in the restaurant had been assembled to ensure the bridal party of four were easily visible to the guests, and the food, comprising several courses, was superb.

There were two speeches: one which Sloane delivered welcoming Georgia into the family, and the other a response from Trenton.

The wedding cake was an exquisite work of art, with intricately iced orchids so incredibly lifelike that one almost wanted to touch a petal to see if it was authentic.

When it was cut, sliced and handed to each guest, Sloane bit into his before feeding some of it to Suzanne in a sensual display she opted to return, for the benefit of their audience. Or so she told herself, for there was a part of her that wished it were real.

The kiss was something else. Evocative and incredibly thorough; there was absolutely nothing she could do about it without causing a stir.

When he lifted his head she could only look at him with a measure of reflected hurt, and just for a second she thought she glimpsed regret beneath the gleaming purpose, then it was gone.

The music changed and Trenton led Georgia onto the floor to dance.

'We'll follow suit,' Sloane indicated, rising to his feet and catching her hand in his.

Now *this*...this was dangerous, she mused as she moved into his arms. It was like coming home. Heaven. Her body fitted his with intimate familiarity, and she felt it quiver in recognition of something beyond which she had little control.

Sexuality. Heightened sensuality. Potent alchemy. If love was like a river, then theirs ran deep. And fast.

She was acutely aware of her own response and, held close like this, she found it impossible to ignore the evidence of desire in his.

It was all she could do not to link her hands together at his nape, and her eyes held bemusement as his lips trailed to one temple.

Suzanne heard her mother's soft laugh, and Sloane's hold loosened as each couple came to a brief halt in order to switch partners.

'It's a beautiful wedding,' Suzanne commented as

124

124 THE BRIDAL BED

Trenton led her into another waltz. Other guests began to join them on the floor.

'Georgia is a beautiful woman. On the inside, where it counts,' he said gently. 'As you are.'

It was a lovely compliment. 'Thank you.'

'I can promise to take good care of her.'

'I know.' It was nothing less than the truth. 'Just as I know you'll both be very happy together.'

They circled the floor again, then Sloane effected the change. Five minutes later another guest cut in, and during the ensuing hour Suzanne danced with almost every man in the room.

Bettina manoeuvred things very skilfully so that she got to dance with Sloane. Suzanne saw each move the glamorous blonde made, and had to commend her tactics.

To anyone else in the room Bettina looked a vivacious guest, and their fleeting attention would have admired the practised smile, the faint flutter of perfectly manicured lacquered nails.

Suzanne, whose examination was much more precise, saw the subtle promise in Bettina's almost-green eyes, the apparent accidental brush of her generous and silicone-enhanced breasts, the inviting part of those perfectly painted lips, and had to still the desire to tear Bettina's eyes out.

Three minutes, four? They each seemed to acquire a tremendous magnitude before Sloane executed a change in partners and drew Suzanne close.

She held herself stiffly within the circle of his arms,

and she moved her head slightly so that his lips brushed her ear and not her cheek as he intended.

'Bettina,' Sloane drawled with stunning accuracy.

'You're *so* perceptive.'

'It's an inherent trait,' he declared musingly. 'Do you know you quiver when you're angry?'

Quiver? 'Really?' She wanted to hit him.

'Which one of us did you want to tear limb from limb?'

'Bettina,' she declared with soft vehemence, and heard his husky chuckle.

'Claws, when there's absolutely no need?'

'Careful,' Suzanne warned. 'I haven't sheathed them yet.'

She leaned into him a little, and heard the strong beat of his heart, felt the strength of his body, and enjoyed the moment for as long as the slow music lasted. Then she joined Georgia and Trenton for a few minutes before slipping to the powder-room to freshen up.

When she returned most of the couples had drifted off the floor to sit in groups at various tables. Sloane was deep in conversation with Bettina's husband, Frank, and Suzanne made her way out onto the terrace where a breeze teased its way in from the ocean.

At this time of year the tropical far north was close to perfection. Lovely sunny days, cool clear nights, and little or no rain. Ideal for those who lived in southern states where winter tended to be cold and wet with winds that gusted round corners and buffeted buildings.

In two days Georgia would fly to Paris. The city for lovers, with its historic buildings and magnificent art collections. Haute couture, food, the total ambience. She'd read about it, viewed the travel documentaries on film, and felt vaguely envious.

No, that wasn't strictly true. There were always goals in life, some achievable, others merely dreams. The aim was to strive for the dream, but not lose sight of the reality.

There was also avarice and greed, which she deplored, along with artificial superficiality. And those who sought and fought for it. Love had been destroyed, lives wrecked, even lost, in pursuit of an abundance of wealth and all it could provide.

A slight shiver shook her slim frame. She'd tasted it, felt the fear and opted to remove herself from its orbit. Had she been right to handle it herself? The doubts, ever present, rose to the surface.

'Voluntary solitude, or an escape?'

Suzanne straightened at the sound of Sloane's drawled query, and she didn't move as he slid his arms round her waist and drew her back against him.

'A little of both,' she answered honestly.

'Want to share?'

Her eyes sprang open at that quietly voiced query. Share her innermost thoughts? That would give the *danger* a new dimension.

'I'll take a rain check.'

She felt his chin rest down on top of her head. 'You realise I'll call it in?'

Yes, he would. But not now. 'Perhaps we should go inside.'

'I came out to find you,' Sloane said. 'Trenton and Georgia intend to retire soon.'

'Leaving the guests to party on?' Was it that late?

'It's almost midnight.'

Where had the evening gone? 'Time flies when you're having fun,' she said lightly, and felt her stomach curl as Sloane moved one hand towards her breast while the other splayed across her hip.

They were, she knew, visible to the guests inside. 'Don't. Please,' she added quietly.

'Then come indoors, and bid our respective parents goodnight.'

Out of the way of temptation. But not for long. Sooner or later they'd return to their villa. What then? She couldn't afford the ecstasy of one long night of loving, or the resulting agony when she had to leave him.

Without a word she slipped free of his hold and led the way indoors.

'Oh, there you are, darling,' Georgia said warmly. 'Trenton and I are about to leave.' She leant forward and gave her daughter a fond hug. 'It's been a splendid party, hasn't it?'

'Really lovely,' Suzanne agreed as she caught hold of her mother's hands.

'Most of the guests are meeting around nine for a champagne breakfast. You'll join us, of course.'

'Of course, Mama.'

'Now we're going to get out of here,' Trenton declared as he bestowed upon his new wife a look of passionate warmth.

Georgia's eyes held a delightful sparkle, and her cheeks bore the faintest tinge of colour.

Trenton took care of their escape by simply declaring, 'Goodnight,' and led Georgia from the restaurant.

'Would you like me to get you some coffee?' Sloane queried.

'Please,' Suzanne replied, and within seconds of his return they were joined by Bettina, which, Suzanne decided, was stretching coincidence a bit far.

'Frank doesn't want to stay and party on. We thought we might go for a walk along the beach. Maybe go for a swim. Want to join us?'

And watch Bettina strip down to nothing and display those voluptuous curves, cavort in the moonlight and attempt to capture more than one man's attention?

'Thanks, but no.' Sloane tempered the refusal with a quizzical smile, then cast Suzanne a dark, gleaming look. 'We have other plans.'

'A party?'

'For two,' he responded evenly. He took Suzanne's cup and saucer and deposited them down onto a nearby table, then he caught hold of her hand. 'If you'll excuse us?'

'We should,' Suzanne admonished mildly, 'say goodnight to the guests.'

'We shall. Very briefly.'

'And have them speculate why we're in such a hurry to leave?'

'Do you want to stay?'

Not really. But she wasn't sure she wanted to go back to the villa, either. Nor did she want to walk along the beach and encounter Bettina.

'No.'

Ten minutes later Sloane unlocked their door, then closed it behind them. Suzanne watched as he shrugged off his suit jacket and draped it over a nearby chair, tugged free his tie and loosened the top two buttons of his shirt.

Then he crossed to the bar-fridge, extracted a magnum of champagne, opened it, filled two flutes, then handed her one. He touched the rim of her flute with his own, then lifted it in silent salute before sipping the contents.

Suzanne was acutely aware of him, and the raw, primitive chemistry that was his alone. There was a brooding sensuality apparent that fired a deep answering need inside her.

She could almost *feel* the blood move more quickly through her veins, the fine hairs on her skin rise as sensitised nerve-ends came alive, and slow heat radiated throughout her whole body.

Imagining how it would be with him almost brought her to a state of climax. Three weeks seemed an eternity, each night apart so long and lonely she'd lain awake aching in solitary pain.

CHAPTER EIGHT

SLOANE glimpsed the faint fleeting shadows, determined their cause, and fought the urge to sweep Suzanne into his arms. The sex would be a wonderful release…for both of them. Wild, wanton, and uninhibited. He could almost smell the bloom of sensual heat on her skin, taste her exotic scent. The thought of sinking into her, hearing the soft purr in her voice change to something deep and driven, the cries of ecstasy as he took her with him…

'It was a lovely wedding.' She had the feeling she'd already said those words, and fought to keep the wistfulness out of her voice, the awkward hesitancy. Dammit, it must be the champagne's eroding effect on her self-confidence. Warm and fuzzy wasn't a feeling she wanted to cultivate. 'Georgia looked radiant.'

'Yes, she did.'

'And Trenton—'

'Wouldn't allow anything or anyone to interfere with their plans,' Sloane interceded. He was silent for a few long seconds, and when he spoke his voice held an inflexible edge. 'Any more than I will.'

There was something in his eyes, the powerful set of his features that triggered alarm bells in her brain. She regarded him carefully, apprehension uppermost as it merged with sickening knowledge. 'You've discovered who she is, haven't you?'

His expression hardened, muscles sculpting broad facial bones into a daunting mask. 'Yes. I had the answer I needed this morning.'

Suzanne didn't have to ask *how*. He had the power and the contacts to elicit any information he wanted. It was impossible to believe that he wouldn't take action. 'What are you going to do?'

'It's already done. Zoe's father is now aware of the facts. And extremely grateful we've chosen not to prosecute. He will personally ensure she seeks professional help.'

Her eyes searched his, and she almost died at the ruthlessness apparent. There was something else she couldn't define, and it frightened her.

'No one,' Sloane intoned with brutal mercilessness, 'threatens me. Directly, or indirectly.' He kept his anger under tight rein. The e-mail report had listed extensive repairs to her car. He could only imagine the verbal assault.

Suzanne saw his clenched fists, evidenced the cold fury in those dark eyes, and placed her partly empty flute onto a nearby pedestal.

She needed to get out of this room, away from him, even if it was only briefly. 'I'm going for a walk.'

'Not alone.'

She tilted her head to look at him, uncaring that the conversation had taken a dangerous shift. 'Don't play the heavy, Sloane.' She walked across the room to the door, her anger so intense she knew she'd *hit* him if he tried to stop her.

Outside the darkness seemed like a shroud, and she followed the lit path down to the beach. When she reached the sand she stepped out of her heeled shoes and bent to collect them in one hand.

Sloane was a short distance behind her, and it was all she could do not to throw something at him. If he wanted to follow her, he could. But she was damned if she'd allow him to dictate her actions, or when she'd return to the villa. *If* she returned, she decided darkly. There were plenty of beach loungers that would make an adequate place to rest for what remained of the night.

The moonlight bathed the beach with an eerie glow, and she trod the crunchy sand to the water's edge, then followed its curve towards the outcrop of rocks.

The tide eddied and flowed at her feet, and on impulse she paused, shed her clothes and dropped them onto dry sand, then turned and walked into the sea.

The water felt silky and wonderfully cool against her skin, and when it reached her waist she eased into a lazy breast-stroke parallel to the shore. Then she turned onto her back and floated, idly counting the sprinkle of stars.

A faint splash alerted her bare seconds before Sloane's dark head appeared less than a metre away.

He didn't say a word, didn't need to, and she moved away from him and rose to her feet. If he was intent on invading her space, then she'd simply shift it somewhere else!

She had only taken two steps towards the shore when hard hands grasped hold of her shoulders and turned her back to face him. 'Let me—'

Anything else she might have said remained locked in her throat as his mouth closed over hers in a kiss that *possessed*...mind, body and soul.

She tried to struggle, and got nowhere. Dear Lord, he was strong. If she could only bite him...but his jaw had possession of her own, dictating its movements as he ravaged the inner tissues with his tongue, his teeth, in a deliberate assault on her senses.

One hand curved down to cup her bottom, while the other held fast her head. She pummelled his back with her fists, and attempted to kick his shin...with totally ineffectual results.

Just when she thought she couldn't bear any more, he loosened his hold, only to change it as he hefted her over one shoulder and walked out of the sea onto the sand.

'What in *hell* do you think you're doing?'

He bent down and she automatically clutched the back of his waist. And found no purchase.

'Collecting our clothes.'

'Put me down!'

He stood upright, adjusted his hold of her, then calmly strode towards the path. 'No.'

'For heaven's sake,' Suzanne hissed. 'Someone might see us.'

'I don't give a damn.'

'At least give me your shirt.' The request came out as a hollow groan.

'I happen to be holding it in front of a vulnerable part of my anatomy,' he responded drily.

'You'd better pray we make it undetected,' she threatened direly. 'Or I'll never forgive you.'

The path to their villa was reasonably short, but Suzanne was conscious of every step Sloane took until they were safely indoors.

'You fiend! How *dare* you?' She pummelled his back with her fists, and attempted to kick him. 'Put me *down*.'

He kept walking, ascended the steps to the bedroom, paused long enough to toss their clothes onto the bed, then he crossed into the *en suite* and turned on the shower.

'What in sweet hell do you think you're doing?'

'Precisely what it looks like.' He stepped into the shower stall and closed the glass sliding door. Then he pulled her down to stand in front of him.

Without thought she lifted a hand and slapped his jaw. Anger, sheer helpless rage, exuded from every pore, and when she lifted her hand a second time he caught it mid-air in a punishing grip.

'You want to fight, Suzanne?'

'*Yes*, damn you!'

'Then go ahead.' He released her hand and stood still, his arms folded across his chest.

His eyes gleamed darkly, silently daring her to thwart him, and she lashed out, both fists flailing as she connected with his chest, his shoulders, anywhere she could land a punch.

He took each and every one, and only grunted once.

Hot, angry tears filled her eyes, then spilled to run in twin rivulets down to her chin. Her knuckles hurt from where she'd struck strong muscle and sinew. And bone. He didn't move, and her arms slowed, then dropped to her sides.

'Are you done?'

The water lashed his shoulders and coursed down his back, and she turned blindly towards the glass door, only to halt as he prevented her escape.

Without a word he pulled her into his arms, effectively stilling any further struggle.

'Let me go.' To stay like this was madness.

Fingers splayed across the base of her spine began a subtle movement, sufficient to make her breath catch, and she tried to pull away from him without success.

The hand that held her nape slid to capture her head, tilting it so she had no defence against his descending mouth.

She expected a devastating invasion, and was unprepared for the soft slide of his tongue against her own. Teasing, tantalising, he made it a sensual assault as he explored and caressed, encouraging her response in a manner that soon left her weak-willed and malleable.

Uncaring of the consequences, she lifted her arms and twined them round his neck, melting into him as she kissed him back. Slowly, tentatively, then with an increasing urgency that left both of them labouring for breath.

'Please.' *Now.* She didn't think she could wait a

second longer, and an exultant laugh broke free from her throat as he parted her thighs and lifted her high to straddle his waist.

With one supple action he buried himself inside her, and she gloried in the hard, deep thrust that stretched silken tissues to a level where she gasped at his degree of penetration.

For several seconds he remained still, then he began to move, slowly at first, each thrust deeper than the last as he increased the pace until their actions became a synchronised match leading to an explosive climax.

Suzanne had thought she'd experienced every facet of his lovemaking, but this had held a wild quality, almost unbridled, as if he was barely retaining a hold on his emotions.

She could only bury her head against his neck as he cradled her close, his lips warm and evocative as they traced a path across one exposed cheek.

How long they stood like that, she had no idea. Long seconds, *minutes* maybe. Eventually her breathing steadied, and with infinite care he set her down onto her feet.

Then he reached for the soap and slowly lathered every inch of her body before turning his attention to his own.

Suzanne felt as if she wasn't capable of moving, much less uttering a single word, and when he switched off the water she stepped out from the shower stall and caught up a towel, only to have him take it from her to blot their skin free of moisture.

Not once did his eyes leave hers, and she became

lost in the darkness, every cell flaring brilliantly *alive* in the knowledge of what would follow.

She wanted him. Dear heaven, so much. But what about afterwards? How could she board the launch on Monday and return to Sydney, her own apartment, and attempt to get on with her life as if this weekend had never happened?

It would be a living nightmare of unfulfilled needing, wanting...*empty*. She doubted if she could survive.

'Sloane—' She couldn't say the words, and she lifted a hand then let it fall helplessly down to her side.

He brushed gentle fingers against her cheek, then let them drift to trace the pulsing cord at her neck.

She was melting inside, subsiding into a state of sensual inertia where all she wanted was for him to continue until the slow warmth heated to white-hot fire.

He knew. She could see it in his eyes, feel it in his touch as his hand slid to her breast and caressed the soft contours before wreaking havoc with the sensitive peak.

His head lowered and his mouth closed over hers in a deep evocative kiss that tore what little defences she had left to shreds. His mouth left hers and followed a sensual path to her breast, savouring, suckling on the tender nub as she arched her neck in silent invitation.

One night, she groaned silently. Just one night.

Her hands reached for him, the movement compulsive as she began exploring tight muscle and sinew, touching, tasting, and wanting more. So much more.

The blood flowed through her veins like quicksilver, feeding every nerve-cell until her whole body ached with need. Sensual heat at its zenith.

Sloane carried her into the bedroom and sank down with her onto the bed. She looked magnificent, her eyes deep blue crystalline, her soft mouth slightly swollen and parted from his kiss. There was a faint sheen on her skin, and her hair hung in tousled disarray.

She leaned forward and initiated a deep kiss, enjoying the feeling of power as he allowed her free rein. Then in one smooth movement she arched her body and took him deep inside, gasping faintly as she felt inner tissues stretch to accommodate him.

Dear God, he felt good. *This* was so good, the feeling of completeness, the joining of two bodies in perfect accord. Sensation spiralled, and she began to move, creating a deep penetrating rhythm as old as time.

His hands reached for her waist, and he joined in the ride, taking her higher and higher until she cried out her release.

Slowly she raised her head and looked down at him, met the dark, slumberous depths and defined the degree of passion evident.

Extending a hand, she touched a gentle finger to his lower lip and traced its outline, then slid it down his chin to his throat, trailing a central line past his chest, his stomach, to where they were still joined, before travelling a similar path to her own mouth.

Slow, sweet warmth swirled deep within, heating her body, and she gave a soft laugh as his hands reached up to bring her head down to his.

This time there was no gentleness in his kiss. It became a foray that was claim-staking, possession at its most damnable as she met and matched the dramatic primitiveness that lay deep within him.

It transcended mere sexual gratification. It was much more than sensual satiation.

A faint groan emerged from her throat as he shifted position and rolled so that she lay on her back.

The control was his, and she wrapped her legs round his hips and pulled him down to her, glorying in his strength.

Afterwards she could only lie still, unable to move as he let his fingers drift idly over the softness of her skin.

She must have slept, for she came awake to the touch of his lips exploring the delicate contours of her body, tasting the spent bloom on her skin as he trailed lower to savour the intimate heart of her.

A banked flame flared into pulsating life, licking through her veins, igniting nerve-ends as she came achingly alive. Consummate skill took her high and tipped her over the edge, and she cried out as she fell.

Afterwards she pleasured him, exulting in the faint sheen of sweat that heated his skin, the quivering muscles of his stomach, the way his breath caught in his throat.

For much of what remained of the night, they indulged in lovemaking, creating a sensual ecstasy that was alternately wild and untamed and slow and evocative.

Suzanne didn't want the magic to end. With the dawn came sleep, and afterwards a long, lingering loving that was so incredibly gentle it made her want to weep.

'We should shower and go down to breakfast,' she said reluctantly as she swept a glance to the digital radio clock.

Sloane's eyes held a mocking gleam that didn't fool her in the slightest. 'Should we?'

'I think so.'

He touched her mouth with his own, savoured its inner sweetness, then trailed soft kisses along the softly swollen contours of her lower lip. 'Why is that?'

Assertiveness was the key. Definitely. For to stay here any longer would be a madness she could ill afford. 'Because I'm hungry.' His eyes became dark and slumberous. 'For food. Sustenance,' she elaborated with an impish grin. 'And I'd almost kill for a cup of strong coffee.' She slid to her feet, stretched her arms high…and felt the pull of muscles. 'I'll hit the shower first.' She directed him a faintly wry glance. 'Alone. Otherwise we'll never get out of here.'

He reached out a hand and pulled her back down to him for a brief, hard kiss, then he let her go. 'Five minutes, then I join you.'

*   *   *

It was almost nine when they entered the restaurant, and Suzanne chose a table on the terrace, ordered coffee, then helped herself to a selection of fresh fruit and cereal from the smorgasbord.

'You're looking rather fragile this morning, darling. Had a hard night?'

She turned and met Bettina's deliberately guileless smile, and proffered one of her own. 'Surely that's rather a personal question?'

'Why pretend? I have my eye on a magnificent emerald and diamond ring.' Her eyes glittered acquisitively. 'Frank needs a little persuasion to buy it for me.'

'Which you have every intention of providing.'

'Why, of course. Women have traded sexual favours for gifts since—*forever*.' Bettina's lashes swept wide. 'Aren't you working hard to persuade Sloane to buy you a Porsche Carrera?'

'*Repaying* me will become a lifetime commitment.'

Suzanne turned at the sound of Sloane's drawling voice, caught his faintly wry, musing smile, glimpsed the dark gleam in his eyes, and opted to respond in kind.

'Not necessarily. My tastes are simple.'

'So are mine,' he said solemnly. '*You.*'

Her pulse tripped and raced to a faster beat. He saw the evidence of it in the hollow at the base of her throat, the dilation of those sapphire depths, the soft parting of her lips.

'The Porsche was meant to be a joke,' she said as she carried her plate back to their table.

'I know.'

'If you gave me one,' she declared fiercely, 'I'd hand it straight back.'

Sloane sank into his chair and ordered fresh coffee. 'I do believe you would.'

'Sloane—'

'You think I don't know Bettina enjoys making mischief?' His dry, mocking tone was matched by a hardness in his eyes.

She was all too aware of the tensile steel beneath the sophisticated veneer. Only a fool would believe he wasn't aware of every angle, and adept in determining the foibles of human nature.

'She has her eye on you.'

His soft laughter brought a fiery sparkle to her eyes. 'Bettina needs confirmation of her attraction to the opposite sex. Her choice of clothes, make-up, jewellery is a blatant attempt at attention-seeking.' His expression assumed a degree of cynicism. 'Any man will do.'

'I disagree,' Suzanne declared as she reached for her coffee. 'That should amend to any well-connected, wealthy man.' She lifted her cup, took an appreciative sip, then replaced it back on its saucer and cast him a wry look. 'And you're more sought after than most.'

'But spoken for,' Sloane asserted tolerantly.

'"A hunk" were her exact words,' she continued as if he hadn't spoken.

'Really?'

He was amused, damn him. 'Definitely *mistress* material.'

'Now why,' he drawled lazily, 'would I covet a mistress, when I have you?'

Suzanne took the time to spear a segment of fresh fruit, which she savoured, then slowly chewed and swallowed, before voicing a response. She chose her words with care, and tempered them with a faint smile. 'You don't *have* me.'

He placed his fork down carefully on his plate, then leant back in his chair, looking, she decided, indolently relaxed and not poised to deliver a verbal sally. 'I retain a particularly vivid memory of how we spent the night.' His dark brown eyes held gleaming humour. 'And the early dawn hours.'

So did she. So much so that it was all she could do to contain the stain of colour spreading high on each cheek. 'I don't think that's entirely relevant.'

She saw one eyebrow lift to form a mocking arch. 'No? I beg to disagree.'

'It was just sex.' Albeit very good sex, she acknowledged silently. And knew she lied. *Sex* didn't even begin to describe what they'd shared.

'I think I should take you back to bed,' Sloane drawled with musing mockery. 'It's the one place where we're in perfect accord.'

She captured another portion of fruit with her fork. 'Our absence would be noticed.'

His regard was warm and infinitely sensual. 'I fail to see that as a problem.'

'You possess a one-track mind,' she admonished him, and reached for her coffee once more.

'Three weeks' abstinence tends to have that effect on a man.'

Not only a man. Even thinking about what they'd shared through much of the night was enough to flood her veins with telling warmth.

The damnable thing was that he knew. The knowledge was apparent in the way his eyes lingered on her mouth, then slid slowly to the heavily beating pulse at the edge of her neck, the slight thrust of each breast.

'I think,' she began, hating the faint raggedness in her voice, 'I've had enough to eat.'

'Georgia and Trenton have just arrived,' Sloane advised quietly, 'and indicated they'll join us.'

The meal became a leisurely affair with the connotation of a champagne brunch as the champagne flowed and staff provided a selection of finger food.

'Tennis this afternoon, definitely,' Georgia declared as she sipped a second cup of black coffee. 'And I think I'll just have fruit for lunch, or forgo it altogether.'

'Likewise.' Followed by a swim, and a nap on the beach, Suzanne decided. A lazily spent afternoon was just what she needed. After last night.

An arrow of pain pierced her body. What of tonight? Would Sloane...? Yes, a silent voice taunted. Of course he will. How would she survive another night of loving without breaking into a thousand pieces? Perhaps if she explained, maybe pleaded with him...

She spared him a quick glance, and then wished she hadn't. His gaze was focused on her features, reading each and every fleeting expression...with damning accuracy, unless she was mistaken.

Did anyone else guess she was a mass of nervous tension beneath the composed exterior? After last night the boundaries she'd imposed had been moved, and she was unsure of their position.

What would happen when she returned to Sydney? *No*, don't think about it, she told herself. *Thinking* wasn't a good idea, for there were just two scenarios. Neither of which she wanted to explore right now.

Her stomach executed a series of painful somersaults, and she forcibly controlled her breathing into a steady, regulated rise and fall. Her heart felt heavy in her chest, and she was sure her contribution to the conversation sounded terribly inane.

In a way it was a relief to circulate among the guests, to lose herself, even briefly, in a social exchange with women whose main topics of conversation seemed to be whose hairdresser was the best, which fashion designer would take out the annual award, and whose parties on the social circuit were *de rigueur* for the remainder of the winter season.

Sloane seemed similarly immersed with Trenton's, and doubtless his own, associates. Twice she glanced in his direction only to have him meet her gaze.

'No hint of a date yet, Suzanne?' one woman asked, while another ventured,

'Paul and I have a very tight schedule until Christmas. Get those invitations out early, darling.'

'You *must* visit Stefano; he'll do wonders with your

hair,' an elegant brunette assured Suzanne, and a glossy dark-haired sylph advised,

'Marie-Louise is without equal for the nails.'

'Gianfranco,' the stylish redhead insisted. 'You must see him about your dress, darling. Tell him Claudia sent you.'

'Of course, there is only O'Neil for the flowers.'

'Frank spent almost a million on my reception,' Bettina offered, and didn't notice the electric silence that followed her announcement.

Suzanne sensed their momentary withdrawal, and their disapproval. Any mention of actual amounts of money among the upper social echelon was *de trop*. One could mention the yacht, the villa in France, the apartment in Venice, Rome or Milan. The Swiss chalet, the New York Fifth Avenue apartment, the London Knightsbridge town house or the mansion in Surrey. *Anything*, except how much it cost. Unless it was an outrageous bargain. Delusions of grandeur were not entertained among society's élite.

It was almost eleven when the guests departed to board the launch that would transfer them to Dunk Island to connect with their flight south.

Suzanne and Sloane joined Georgia and Trenton on the jetty to see them off.

CHAPTER NINE

'Now I can relax.' Georgia wound an arm round Trenton's waist and leaned in against him. 'It's been a wonderful weekend. Thank you, darling.'

The look he directed at her mother brought a lump to Suzanne's throat. So much love, so clearly visible. It made her heart ache. 'I don't think I could eat or drink a thing,' she declared lightly. 'I'm going to take a book down onto the beach, then go for a dip in the ocean.'

'We'll meet for tennis,' Trenton indicated. 'Four o'clock, OK?'

'You could,' Sloane drawled minutes later as they entered their villa, 'relax here.'

Suzanne twisted her head to look at him. 'Uh-uh. I don't think our ideas of *relaxation* match.' She ran quickly up the steps to the bedroom and extracted a black bikini.

'Afraid to be alone with me?'

He posed a tremendous threat to her equilibrium, but *fear* had no part in it. 'No.'

Sloane crossed to her side and placed his hands at the base of her nape, initiating a soothing massage that felt so good...too damned good. 'Tired?'

She wanted to close her eyes and sink back against him, have him hold her, kiss her. Slow, oh, so slowly.

147

If she gave in to such feelings, they'd never get out of the villa before nightfall.

'A little.'

'Let me indulge you,' he commanded quietly.

Need curled deep inside her, then twisted into a spiral that radiated through her body. Her smile was incredibly sad, and tinged with regret. 'I don't think that's such a good idea.'

His breath feathered her temple. 'No?'

His fingers skimmed beneath the hair at her nape, lifting it aside as he traced his lips down to the sensitive spot behind one ear, savoured it, then trailed the pulsing cord to the edge of her neck.

'Sloane.' The protest fell from her lips in scarcely more than an agonised whisper as his fingers loosened tight shoulder muscles.

'Shh,' he bade her gently. 'Just relax.'

Dared she? Maybe just for a few minutes. There was no harm in just a few minutes, surely?

Suzanne closed her eyes and let all her muscles relax as he began weaving a subtle magic that seemed to seep into her very bones.

She was hardly aware of him sliding the zip free at the back of her dress, or the faint slither as it slipped to the floor. Her bra clasp undid with ease, and his hands smoothed her slip down over her hips.

'I don't think—'

'Don't *think*,' Sloane said huskily. 'Just feel.'

His lips tasted her skin, embraced it, and roamed at will over her neck, her shoulders, then trailed down one arm to the sensitive hollow at her elbow, before tracing the delicate veins down to the inside of her wrist.

A despairing groan escaped her throat as he rendered a similar treatment to the other arm, and when he turned her into his arms she had no will of her own to prevent him laying her gently down on the bed.

What followed was a long, slow supplication of every pleasure point, each pulse. The curve of her hip, the inside of one thigh, the hollow behind each knee. The sensitive slope of her calf, the tender hollows at her ankle, the acutely vulnerable arch of her foot.

She felt as if she was slowly dying as pleasure radiated from every pore, each nerve-cell, as his hands, his lips roved at will. Her breasts, their sensitised peaks, the soft concave of her stomach. The rapidly discolouring bruise at her hip. Nothing escaped his attention.

Her blood leapt as he brushed the most intimate crevice of all, and her limbs slid against the sheet in agitation, then her whole body jerked as he began effecting a simulation of the sexual act itself.

His hands cupped her hips and held them as he wreaked a havoc that was so incredibly tender, so intensely evocative, her body seemed to sing as one vibration after another shook her central core and radiated in all-consuming waves.

He felt her shudder in release, and gifted her an open-mouthed kiss before travelling a slow path to her waist, then the soft contour of one breast.

It was a torturous journey until his mouth reached hers, and the kiss was so gentle she felt the prick of tears and their warm spill as they trickled slowly across each cheekbone and disappeared into her hair.

Sloane felt the faint tremor as her body shook, and he lifted his head fractionally, glimpsed the drenched sapphire pools and removed the trail of moisture with his tongue.

Then he stretched out close and gathered her in against him. 'Better?'

Dear Lord, did he have any conception of how she felt? 'There's only one problem,' she murmured shakily.

His fingers brushed against her cheek. 'What's that?'

Her mouth trembled as she reached for him. 'You're wearing too many clothes.'

His smile was infinitely warm and sensual. 'You could have fun taking them off.'

'Is that an invitation?'

Lips traced the clean line of her jaw. 'Do you need one?'

This was special. Something so precious, the memory would last her for the rest of her life. Through all the lonely, empty nights, an inner voice sighed in sorrow.

His shoes came first, then she took time with the buckle of his trousers, the zip fastening, silently encouraging his help as she slid the garment free. Undoing each shirt button became a tantalising exercise as her fingers tangled with the springy hair curling in a sparse pattern across his tightly muscled chest.

All that remained was a pair of silk briefs, and she traced the waistband as it stretched across his hipbone, the firm plane of his stomach, and allowed her fingers to brush fleetingly over his arousal.

Control. He had it. Part of her wanted to see what it would take to break it as she tucked her fingers into the waistband and eased the briefs free.

With incredible slowness she copied his example, teasing, tasting, glorying in the soft tremor of his stomach, each flexed muscle as she traversed every inch of his body.

The most vulnerable, the most erotic part of his anatomy she left until last, laving it with such delicate artistry, he groaned in the effort to maintain control.

Minutes later his breath rasped in one husky exhalation, and hard hands grasped her shoulders as he rolled her onto her back and drove into her in one deep thrust.

Suzanne gave an exultant laugh and met his mouth as it came down in possession of her own, and together they climbed to each crest as raw, primitive sensation took them high in a mutual climax so devastatingly flagrant there were no words to define it.

Afterwards he cradled her against him as his fingers trailed a soothing pattern up and down her back, tracing each indentation of her spine.

She slept, drifting into blissful somnolence, secure in the knowledge that she was safe. *His*. Undoubtedly his.

Suzanne came awake at the soft pressure of lips brushing against her own, and she opened her eyes slowly, allowing the lashes to drift wide as she focused on the man who was intent on disturbing a dreamy ambience she was loath to leave.

'It's almost four,' Sloane informed her huskily, and she offered him a slow, sweet smile.

'Time to shower, dress, and meet Trenton and Georgia for tennis.'

'I could ring through to their villa and cancel.'

'We shouldn't disappoint them,' she opined solemnly, and he uttered a faint laugh. 'Should we?'

'Witch.' He levered himself off the bed, and extended a hand. 'Come on, then, or we'll be late.'

They were, but only by ten minutes, and Georgia and Trenton were already on the court, quite happily enjoying a relaxing rally.

Together, they agreed on one set, and although both men were evenly matched the pace was laid-back rather than competitive, ending an hour later with a seven-five win in favour of Sloane and Suzanne.

'A drink in the bar?' Sloane suggested as they exited the court, and Trenton clapped a hand to his son's shoulder in silent agreement.

'I must be feeling my age,' Georgia declared with a sparkling laugh as they entered the main complex and sank into comfortable chairs.

Trenton signalled to the waiter and within minutes they were each sipping something long and cool.

'Dinner at six-thirty?' Trenton proposed. 'I'll have someone alert the dining room.'

That would give them time to shower and change. Their final night on the island, Suzanne reflected, unsure whether to feel relieved or regretful that the extended weekend sojourn was almost at an end.

What had begun as something she'd have given anything to avoid had become quite different in many respects from anything she'd envisaged.

The anger, the resentment was gone. Yet what was in its place? The sex was great. Better than great...magnificent. But was that *all* it was?

She wanted to ask, but she was afraid of the answer. *Knew* that if she was to survive emotionally she had to cull some form of self-preservation.

'It'll be the last night we spend with Georgia and Trenton for a while,' Sloane reflected with indolent ease. 'Shall we view a video, play cards, or just take a leisurely stroll along the beach for a while after dinner?'

Trenton looked from his wife to his stepdaughter for confirmation. 'Georgia? Suzanne?'

Georgia's smile was infectious. 'Cards. Suzanne and I are rather good, aren't we, darling?'

It was, Suzanne decided gratefully, the more mentally stimulating choice. 'Yes,' she conceded with droll humour. 'Let's pit our combined skills and see if we can beat them.'

Sloane arched an eyebrow and spared his father a wry look. 'Men against the women?'

Trenton indulged in a husky chuckle. 'You do play, Sloane? Otherwise we're in deep trouble.'

'Your villa or ours?'

'Yours,' Trenton drawled, and shot Georgia a wicked glance. 'Then we can leave when we want to.'

'Bring matchsticks,' Suzanne bade them solemnly. 'Georgia and I never play for money.'

They finished their drinks and wandered out into the cool evening air. Darkness was falling, and already the garden lights illuminated the complex and grounds.

Trenton and Georgia paused at a fork in the path leading to their villa. 'We'll meet in the restaurant in half an hour.'

Once indoors, Suzanne made straight for the *en suite*, stripped off her clothes, and stepped beneath the warm pulsing water. Then gasped in surprise when Sloane followed close behind her.

His presence triggered a spiral of electric energy, and she reached for the soap only to have it removed from her hand.

What followed became an incredibly sensual assault that heightened every nerve-ending until her entire body seemed to pulse with sensory awareness.

When he finished he silently handed her the soap, and she returned his ministrations, then stood still as he rinsed the lather from his skin.

He reached for the water dial and closed it, then he cupped her face and kissed her hard and all too briefly before reaching out for a towel.

'I don't think we need dress up. Something casual will do.'

Nevertheless she did, selecting black silk evening trousers and a matching silk singlet top. She kept make-up to a minimum, and added a slim gold chain

Georgia had gifted her on her twenty-first birthday. Medium-heeled strappy sandals completed the outfit.

Wearing immaculate ivory linen trousers and a deep blue cotton shirt, Sloane exuded a vibrant energy that was intensely male, and her senses leapt when he enfolded her hand in his as they made their way to the restaurant.

Dinner was a convivial meal, and they each chose locally caught seafood, garnished with a variety of fresh salad greens. They opted out of dessert and selected the cheeseboard instead, with fresh grapes and cantaloupe, followed by a sinfully rich liqueur coffee.

A leisurely walk among the lamp-lit grounds and gardens extended the time it took to reach the villa, and once inside they seated themselves comfortably at the table while Trenton extracted and shuffled a pack of cards.

It wasn't so much the game, or winning, Suzanne mused as she collected the cards she'd been dealt. She found the pitting of mental skills honed by chance to be an enjoyable challenge. Predicting how the suits and the numbers would run, and the odds. She didn't believe in tricks, or sleight of hand, and abhorred players who utilised any system.

As a pair, she and Georgia won the first game, then the second. When the third meant another loss for the men, there was keen speculation about the fourth game.

'I think we're about to go down,' Trenton declared, meeting Sloane's musing smile with one of his own.

'If we win, we'll split up and change partners,' Georgia offered generously.

'Now that could make things interesting,' Sloane drawled, and Suzanne spared him a wicked grin.

'Must we, Mama? This might be the only advantage we'll ever gain over them.'

Sloane lifted a hand and brushed his knuckles across her cheek. 'Oh, I don't know,' he intoned tolerantly. 'I can think of other advantages.' His eyes were dark with lambent warmth, his meaning unmistakable, and there was absolutely nothing she could do about the soft tinge of colour that flared high across her cheekbones.

'You'll embarrass my mother,' she chided, and Trenton laughed.

'Doubtful, darling,' Georgia assured her.

Suzanne looked from one gleaming gaze to another, and conceded defeat. 'I think we should play on.' Afterwards, when they were alone, she'd pay Sloane back. And relish every second of it. She shot him a silently threatening glance from beneath her lashes, and glimpsed the teasing gleam in those dark depths.

It gave her a degree of satisfaction to win, and she chose to be paired with Trenton against Georgia and Sloane in a series of games that brought a finish so close, the margin was minuscule in Georgia and Sloane's favour.

Being seated opposite him provided the opportunity to watch every move, glimpse each facial expression, the faint narrowing of his eyes as he considered which card to play, which one to discard.

He was a superb tactician, a supreme strategist. And he learned really fast. Too fast. It made her wonder if he hadn't deliberately played to lose earlier.

'Anyone for coffee?'

'No, thank you, darling.' Georgia spared a glance at her watch, then rose to her feet. 'We'll see you at breakfast. Around eight?'

Sloane walked at Suzanne's side to the door. 'We'll be there.'

Georgia leaned forward and brushed her daughter's cheek with her own. 'Sleep well.'

As soon as the door had closed behind them, Suzanne crossed to the table and gathered up the pile of matchsticks, then collected the cards.

'Leave them.'

His smile was warm with implied intimacy, and she almost melted at its mesmerising quality. 'It'll only take a minute. Then I'll pack.'

His expression didn't change. 'There's plenty of time to do that in the morning.'

She looked at him helplessly. 'Sloane—' How could she say she was a mass of nerves, relieved in one way the weekend was almost over, yet deep inside fighting off a feeling of inconsolable grief? Wanting him, but reluctant to add another night of loving that would only add to the heartache? She shook her head in silent remonstrance, then drew on inner strength. 'It won't take long.'

He was close, much too close. Her breathing seemed to hang suspended as her pulse raced into overdrive.

'Look at me.'

Her stomach executed a painful flip. 'Sloane—'

'Look at me, Suzanne,' he commanded in a voice that was deceptively mild—too mild.

She turned from her task of clearing the table, and hugged her arms together in an involuntary defensive gesture.

'You're as skittish as a newborn foal.' And consumed by a confusing mix of contrary emotions, he added silently, aware of almost every one of them. 'Want to talk about *why*?'

How did she begin, and *where*? Or should she even begin at all? *Words* seemed superfluous and contradictory, yet there were things that needed to be said.

She looked at his strongly etched features, and felt as if she was teetering on the edge of a bottomless pit.

'I'd like to go to bed. It's late, and I'm tired.'

He reached out a hand and took hold of her chin, then tilted it. 'You're avoiding the issue.'

Her eyes darkened, and she felt them begin to ache with suppressed emotion. 'Tomorrow we go back to Sydney and lead separate lives.'

'If you believe I'm going to let that happen, then you're sadly mistaken.'

He lowered his head and angled his mouth over hers in a gentle possession that soon hardened into something deep and incredibly erotic.

It was all she could do not to respond, and she fought against the dictates of her own traitorous body, almost hating herself for being so mindless, so incredibly vulnerable where he was concerned.

Want; need. The two were entwined, yet separate. With differing meanings, depending on the gender.

A man could want, and use seducing skills to achieve sexual satisfaction. Was that what Sloane was doing? Making the most of the weekend?

Yet it was two-sided. She hadn't exactly displayed too much reluctance.

When he lifted his head she could only stand in silence, her eyes wide and hiding her pain.

His arm slid down her back, and she tried to put some distance between them. Without success. 'Please, don't.'

'Don't *what*, Suzanne? Take you to bed? Is that what this is all about?' His eyes searched hers, and glimpsed the slight flaring evident in her own.

'Sex isn't the answer to everything.'

He noted the faint wariness in the set of her beautiful mouth, the bruised softness in those crystalline blue eyes, and wanted to wipe away all the indecision, the doubt, and replace it with the uninhibited emotion she'd gifted him in the beginning.

'I don't call what we share *sex*,' Sloane opined gently.

No, it was never just sex. Shared intimacy, lovemaking, a sensual exploration and satiation of the senses with *love* the ultimate goal.

'Last night—'

'Last night was a mistake.'

His eyes hardened to dark obsidian shards, and his expression became a bleak, angry mask.

CHAPTER TEN

'THE hell it was.'

'Sloane—'

'What excuse are you going to try for, Suzanne? Too much champagne, when you barely touched a second glass? It seemed like a good idea at the time?' His dark eyes bored into her with relentless and deadly anger. 'What?'

Oh, God. She closed her eyes, then opened them again. 'It wasn't like that.'

'Then explain how it was.'

Magical, euphoric. Devastating in more ways than one. She tried for an ineffectual shrug and almost got it right. 'I let the pretence become reality.' The burning need to experience heaven one last time.

'You expect me to believe that?' His voice was dangerously quiet.

'Dammit, Sloane. What do you want? A blow-by-blow analysis of my emotions?'

'The truth might help.'

'What truth?'

'There were two people in that bed. And you were with me every inch of the way.'

'So what does that prove, other than you're a skilled lover?'

'Are you saying you'd respond to any man the way you respond to me?'

No. Never. So deep was her certainty, it robbed the power from her voice.

'Suzanne?'

His eyes sharpened, homing in on the thinly disguised bleakness. 'You didn't answer the question.'

Her eyes blazed, and she lifted her chin to a defiant angle. 'What would you do if I said *yes*?'

His expression frightened her. 'Be tempted to beat you within an inch of your life.'

'You're not a violent man,' she said with certainty, only to have that conviction waver at the brilliant flare of intense emotion evident in his eyes, the deep set of his features projecting a mask that made her feel suddenly afraid. Which was ridiculous.

'Try me.' The silky softness of his voice sent a chill chasing the length of her spine.

Gone was the cool, implacable control of the courtroom barrister. Absent, too, was the veneer of sophistication. In its place was a man intent on fighting—if not physically then verbally—to the bitter end to effect a resolution. Here, now. No matter what the outcome.

Suzanne moved her shoulders in an infinitely weary gesture. 'Can't this wait until morning?' It had been a long night, and an even longer day.

He folded both arms across his chest. 'No.'

'Sloane—'

'No,' he reiterated with dangerous softness.

She was almost at the end of her tether, tired in

spirit, physically, emotionally. All she wanted to do was undress, curl into bed and sleep.

Then, when she woke in the morning, the long weekend would be over. She'd board the launch, take the flight back to Sydney, and attempt to take up with her life again. Without Sloane.

'What do you *want* from me?' It was a tortured cry straight from the heart.

A muscle bunched at the edge of his jaw. 'You. Just you.'

Her throat ached with emotion, and she was willing to swear her heart stopped beating.

'As my wife, my partner, the twin half of my soul. For the rest of my life.'

She could only look at him in silence as she tried to assemble a few words that made sense.

He didn't give her the chance. 'I have a Notice of Intention to Marry in my possession.' He let his arms fall to his sides. 'All you have to do is attach your signature prior to the service tomorrow morning.'

Her voice emerged from her throat with difficulty. 'Tomorrow?' The single query was little more than a soundless gasp. 'Are you mad?'

'Remarkably sane.'

Suzanne felt as if she needed to sit down. 'We can't possibly—'

'We can,' Sloane insisted. 'You're as aware of the legalities as I am.' He paused fractionally, then touched a gentle finger to the corner of her mouth, traced its outline, then let his hand fall. 'Georgia and Trenton will act as witnesses.'

'You expect me to agree to all this?' she questioned weakly.

He looked at her for long, timeless minutes, examining the fall of clean blonde hair, the fine-textured skin with minimum make-up coverage, the beautiful crystalline blue eyes. And played his last card.

'We can go back to Sydney tomorrow and begin organising the *social event of the year*. Plan the date, the venue, the marquee, the guest list, your designer gown, the media. If that's what you want, I'll go along with it. Happily.' He paused, his voice softening. 'As long as it means I get *you*.' He lifted a hand and brushed gentle fingers down her cheek, then cupped her jaw. 'Or we can marry quietly here, tomorrow.' His smile held incredible warmth. 'The choice is yours.'

Life with Sloane. Life without Sloane. There really wasn't any choice at all. Never had been.

'Tomorrow?' she reiterated in stunned disbelief.

'Tomorrow,' Sloane insisted.

Suzanne's brain whirled with numerous implications. 'You planned it like this,' she said unsteadily. 'Didn't you?'

He touched a forefinger to her lips. 'I planned to marry you. The time, the place were irrelevant.'

She searched his features and glimpsed the strength of purpose evident. 'Georgia and Trenton's wedding, this remote island resort—' She faltered, absently lifting a hand to push a lock of hair behind her ear. 'Their plans made it easy for you to—'

'Discover the truth,' he finished.

'But what if—'

There was a faint edge of tension beneath the surface of his control that he fought hard to subdue. Losing her temporarily had nearly cost him his sanity.

'You said you needed time and space,' Sloane declared quietly. 'Something I vowed to give you... within reason.'

Suzanne digested his words, and perceived the meaning behind them. 'You had that much faith in me?'

A slight tremor in her voice brought a faint smile, and he lifted a hand and tucked another loose tendril of hair behind her ear. 'Yes.'

She saw the passion visible in those dark, arresting features, and her bones began to melt. 'Thank you,' she said simply.

His mouth curved with sensual warmth, deepening the darkness of his eyes as he leaned forward and trailed his lips along her cheekbone, then traced her jaw and settled near the edge of her mouth.

Without hesitation she shifted slightly and parted her lips to meet his in a kiss that merged from warmth to flaring heat in the space of a heartbeat.

It seemed an age before he lifted his head. 'We have a wedding to organise.'

Suzanne's eyes gleamed as she sought to tease him a little. 'I don't have anything suitable to wear.'

'Yes, you do.'

In her mind's eye she skimmed the clothes she'd brought with her. 'I do?' The pale blue silk slip dress she'd worn the day before would suffice...providing the resort staff could work a cleaning miracle in time.

'Trust me.'

She opened her mouth, then closed it again.

He smiled, and it sent lines fanning out from the corners of each eye. 'Do I take that to mean a *yes*?'

Suzanne tried for solemnity, and failed. 'It depends what I'm saying *yes* to.'

He leaned forward and brushed his lips to the curve of her neck. His mouth moved lower, trailed a path up her throat and hovered above her lips. He angled his mouth down to hers and took his fill, plundering, possessing, until she could be in no doubt of his feelings, *hers*.

'Marrying me.'

His mouth was intent on wreaking such delicious havoc with her senses, savouring the delicate flavour of her skin, while his hands sought and found the acutely sensitised pleasure spots that drove her wild.

'Tomorrow.'

Yes, she cried silently. There were words she wanted to say, assurances she felt the need to give.

'Sloane.'

His hands stilled at the way her voice caught in saying his name, and his mouth paused in its downward path. He lifted his head and took in the soft fullness of her lips, the dilated depths of her eyes.

'I love you.' Words, just three of them. Yet in saying them she gifted more than her body. Her heart, her soul. Everything.

His hands shook slightly as they slid up to cup her face, and his expression was devoid of any artifice.

Joy, *love*, slow-burning deep emotion. Passion. Just for her.

'Thank you,' he said gently.

The anger, the frustration, the sheer helplessness that had coloured the past few weeks disappeared. He knew he never wanted to experience them again.

No one would ever be permitted to diminish what they shared, or seek to damage it in any way. There would be no more doubts, no room for any insecurity. He would personally see to it. Every day of his life.

Suzanne watched the changing emotions and successfully read every one of them. The resolution, the caring. And love.

His thumb moved across the fullness of her lower lip with a reverence that made her want to cry. 'I'm yours,' he said softly. 'Always.' His lips curved into a slow smile that melted her bones. 'For ever.'

She had to blink rapidly to dispel the suspicious moistness behind her eyes. 'Then I guess we get married tomorrow.' Her mouth moved to form a shaky smile. 'What on earth will Georgia and Trenton think?'

Sloane kissed the tip of her nose. 'Be delighted, I imagine.'

She leaned into him, overwhelmed by the sheer feel and power of him. 'Let's—' She paused slightly as Sloane's hand slid beneath the hem of her top and worked an evocative path towards one hip.

'Make love?' His husky chuckle was low and infinitely sensual.

'Go for a walk along the beach afterwards?' In the moonlight, in the stillness of night, with the sound of water lapping softly against the sand. Enjoying the magic of an island that was removed from civilisation, where solitude and privacy were guaranteed.

'Sure,' Sloane agreed easily.

'Providing you have sufficient energy left, of course,' she said with demure amusement, and had her laugh cut short as his mouth closed over hers in a kiss that promised total ravishment.

'Planning on wearing me out, huh?' he teased as he carried her upstairs, then laid her down on the bed.

As he undressed his eyes were so dark, magnificent. And alive with a passion that made her catch her breath. Slowly, and with a sensuality that wasn't contrived, she lifted the hem of her top, pulled it over her head and dropped it onto the floor.

He eased himself down onto the bed beside her and she lowered her head and kissed his shoulder, trailing her mouth down to one hard male nipple, savoured it, then followed the dark hair arrowing down to his navel.

Beneath the fine black silk briefs his arousal was a potent force, and she caressed its outline with the tip of her tongue. It created a slight friction that made him catch his breath, and with a boldness she didn't pause to question she took the waistband between her teeth and gradually eased them down, inch by inch until the briefs were reduced to a narrow fold across the top of his thighs.

There was a tremendous beauty in the aroused male form, the knowledge of what that harnessed power could achieve in the pleasure stakes. For each of them.

Suzanne felt as if she wanted to laugh and cry, both at the same time, with the intense joy of being with this man, for she couldn't remember feeling so *alive*, so complete. It was like coming home, the knowledge of everything being *right*. She wanted to tell him, show him.

And she did. With infinite care, and a passion unfettered by uncertainty or reservation.

She wasn't sure when Sloane took control. Only that together they experienced emotions at their zenith again and again during the ensuing night hours.

Suzanne stirred as fingers trailed a light path across the flat plane of her stomach, and nuzzled the warm flesh beneath her cheek.

She didn't want to move. Didn't think she *could* move.

'I guess the moonlit walk along the beach will have to wait.'

Suzanne registered Sloane's amused drawl, felt his warm breath tease her temple, and slowly opened her eyes to discover an early dawn fingering soft light into the room.

'Well,' she murmured, 'there's always the early morning swim.'

His soft laughter reverberated beneath her ear, and she lifted her head to look at him, glimpsed the teasing warmth evident in the generous curve of his mouth, the liquid darkness of his eyes, and wrinkled her nose.

'Don't you think I'm capable?'

The corners of his eyes creased, and the darkness intensified. 'I should come along in case you drown.'

'You, of course, are a bundle of energy this fine morning?' She trailed her fingers across his midriff, felt the muscles tighten and created a playful pattern with the dark hair there.

'Go any lower, and I won't answer to the consequences,' Sloane warned huskily.

'Just checking,' she told him with impish mischievousness, then gasped as he lifted her across his chest, rolled her onto her back, and fastened his mouth on hers with devastating accuracy.

She clung to him, meeting his ardour with her own, loving the fierceness before it altered and softened into something that was incredibly gentle.

'A swim,' she said with a shaky smile. 'Definitely a swim. Otherwise we'll never get out of here.'

They rose, donned minimum swimwear, and Suzanne caught up a cotton wrap as Sloane collected a towel.

Outside it was still, and there wasn't a sound. No birdlife, not so much as a breeze to riffle the foliage as they made their way onto the sand.

A new day, she mused, watching as the colours around her gradually intensified. Crisp white sand, the sea changing hue from blue to aqua, clearly defined from an azure sky. The air was warm and devoid of the sun's heat.

As she watched, the golden orb's outer rim crept above the horizon, bringing with it the clarity of light, and she heard the first twitter as birds awoke.

Sloane watched her expressive features, the way her mouth curved slightly open, the softness in those vivid blue eyes as she stood there.

'Want to walk along the shoreline?'

She turned slowly towards him, and her eyes teased his. 'Dip our toes in the water, skim a few shells out over the surface?'

'Commune with Nature, and maybe sacrifice a swim for a long warm shower?'

Suzanne gave a throaty laugh as she caught hold of his hand. 'Chicken,' she teased. 'A bracing cold swim, a hearty breakfast...' She trailed off with a grin. 'Just what we need to kick-start the day.' Her eyes sparkled with humour. 'Last one in—' She didn't get to finish as she was swept off her feet and carried into the water. 'Sloane. Don't you *dare*.'

Cool, not cold, and definitely bracing. The hearty breakfast came way after the long warm shower.

Then things seemed to move very swiftly into action.

The celebrant didn't turn a hair when asked to perform another ceremony. Georgia and Trenton were thrilled with the news. The restaurant management appeared completely unfazed at the request to prepare a small but sumptuous midday wedding feast.

Suzanne gasped out loud when Georgia removed a

pale ivory creation of silk and lace from its protective covering, added shoes, and a fingertip veil.

Sloane's contingency plan.

She reached out a hand and touched the exquisite lace overlay. 'It's beautiful.' The correct size, the right length, perfect.

'Did you—?'

'Help?' Georgia queried. 'No, I swear.'

'You're not going to ask if I have doubts?'

'I don't need to,' her mother said gently. 'You wouldn't be about to do this if you had them.'

No, Suzanne agreed in contemplative silence as she crossed to the mirror and began tending to her make-up.

It was almost eleven-thirty when she made the final adjustment to her veil and stood back from the mirror.

'You take my breath away,' Georgia said with a tremulous smile.

'Don't you dare cry,' Suzanne admonished her with a shaky grin. 'Or I will too, then we'll have to redo our make-up, which will make us late, and Sloane will send Trenton on a rescue mission, only to follow closely on his heels with the celebrant in tow.' Her eyes danced with expressive mischief. 'Not exactly a scene I would choose. Besides, we can't have this hastily arranged service misconstrued as a kidnap attempt of the bride by the groom, can we? Think what a field day the gossip columns would have with that!'

Georgia's mouth quivered as she caught hold of her daughter's outstretched hand. 'Unthinkable,' she agreed solemnly.

Tables had been cleared at one end of the restaurant to make room for an elegant archway threaded with hibiscus and frangipani in brilliant shades of pink. Soft music filtered from a stereo system, and red carpet formed a temporary aisle.

Suzanne took a deep breath, accepted the reassuring squeeze from her mother's fingers, then began walking slowly towards the archway where Sloane and Trenton waited with the celebrant.

Father and son were similar in height and stature, their breadth of shoulder outlined by superb tailoring, and almost in unison both men turned to watch the two women in their lives walk towards them.

Suzanne felt as if time stood still. Her eyes met Sloane's, and clung. Everything else faded to the periphery of her vision as she drew close, and there was him, only him.

The expression in those liquid brown eyes held a warmth that threatened to melt her bones. There was a wealth of emotion apparent as he smiled, and her step almost faltered as she reached his side.

Sloane caught hold of her hand and lifted it to his lips, then he kissed each finger in turn, slowly, as her heart went into overdrive.

She was barely aware that Georgia moved to one side, and she endeavoured to focus on the celebrant's voice as he intoned the words, elicited their individual responses, then solemnly accorded them man and wife after the exchanging of rings.

'You may now kiss the bride.'

Sloane lifted the fine veil with infinite care, then

his hands slid to cup her face, and his head descended as he took possession of her mouth in a kiss that claimed and pleasured with such thoroughness, her skin tinged a delicate pink at the blatant promise apparent.

Afterwards they sipped Cristal champagne from slim crystal flutes, posed for the essential few photographs, then took their seats at an elegantly decorated table where they were served the finest seafood in delicate sauces, fresh salads, an incredible pavlova decorated with fresh cream and fruit for dessert, followed by the pièce de résistance, an iced wedding cake. Which necessitated more champagne, a toast, followed by coffee.

As weddings went, it had to be one of the smallest, most intimate affairs on record, Suzanne mused as they stood and thanked Georgia and Trenton, the staff, the celebrant, then led the way from the restaurant.

Sadly, the romantic idyll was almost over, for in half an hour the launch would leave for Dunk Island, where the family jet was on standby to fly them to Sydney.

Inside the villa Sloane caught hold of her hands and drew her close.

'I don't think we have time for this,' Suzanne said a trifle breathlessly as his head descended to hers.

'Depends on your definition of *this*,' Sloane teased, touching his lips to the corner of her mouth as he trailed a tantalising path along the contours of her lower lip.

A groan escaped her throat, and she angled her

mouth so that it fitted his, encouraging a possession he didn't hesitate to give.

It seemed an age before he lifted his head, and she could only look at him in total bemusement. 'I think,' she managed huskily, 'we should change and pack.'

His lips brushed across her forehead. 'Change, but not pack.' He lingered at her temple, then traced the edge of her jaw. 'We're staying here.'

'How can we stay? I'm due back at work tomorrow.' Her eyes widened. 'You must have court appearances.' Her voice husked down to a mere whisper. 'It's not possible.'

He lifted his head and surveyed her features with musing indulgence. 'Yes, it is.' He placed a forefinger beneath her chin and lifted it. 'All it took was a few phone calls.'

'But you can't—'

'I just have.'

'My job—'

'Secure,' Sloane assured her. 'For as long as you want it.'

She drew in a shaky breath, then released it. 'What did you tell them?'

His thumb traced the column of her throat, felt the convulsive movement as she swallowed, and soothed it with the gentle brush of his fingers. 'The truth.' He explored the hollow at the edge of her neck, and felt her quivering response. 'You have a week's leave with their blessing.'

It was feasible her work could be shared around.

Sloane, however, was in a vastly different position. 'But what about you?'

'Forward planning,' he declared, and effected a slight shrug. 'I did a bit of shuffling, called in a few favours.'

'How long?' It couldn't possibly be more than a day or two.

'I'm not due in court until Friday.'

She wanted to kiss and hug him, both at the same time. 'I love you,' she said reverently. 'Later, I intend to show you just how much.'

'Promises?'

She offered him a brilliant smile. 'Oh, yes. Definitely. But now,' she declared, 'we change, then we'll go see Georgia and Trenton onto the launch.'

His mouth quirked with humour, playing her game. 'And after?'

'A girl's wedding day is special.' Her smile was infinitely wicked. 'Something of which memories are made and reminisced over down the years.' She lifted both hands and ticked off her fingers, one by one. 'There's the champagne, the bridal waltz, and the throwing of the bridal bouquet.' Irrepressible humour intensified the blue of her eyes. 'You planned the first half of the day. Are you willing to leave the second half to me?'

Sloane caught hold of her hands, and kissed the inside of each wrist before releasing them. 'I guess I can do that.'

CHAPTER ELEVEN

THEY reached the jetty a few minutes before Georgia and Trenton, together with the celebrant, were due to board the launch. Goodbyes were affectionate, but brief.

'I want postcards from Paris,' Suzanne insisted gently as she kissed Georgia.

'Done.'

Suzanne stood within the circle of Sloane's arms as the launch moved out of sight, then she turned and curved an arm around his waist.

'Let's walk along the beach.'

He looked down at her expressive features, caught the faint shadows beneath her eyes and experienced a faint pang of regret that he was the cause. She needed to catch up on sleep. Dammit, they both did.

'No rock-climbing,' he warned, and she laughed, a light, infectious sound that curled round his heart.

'Intent on preserving the energy levels?'

The smile he slanted her held warm humour. 'Yours, as well as my own.'

They trod the soft sand to the first promontory, then turned and slowly retraced their steps. The pool looked inviting, and they stroked a few lengths in lazy rhythm before emerging to lie supine side by side on two loungers, allowing the soft warm breeze to dry the brief, thin pieces of silk they each wore.

Suzanne must have slept, for she dreamt of isolated incidents that had no common linkage, and woke to the drift of fingers tracing a soft pattern down her forearm.

The sun was low in the sky, and there were long shadows deepening the colour of the sand.

'It's late.'

'Does it matter?' Sloane queried, propping himself up on one arm.

She rose to her feet in one fluid movement. 'We have a dinner reservation in half an hour.' She stretched a hand towards him. 'Time to rise and shine and shower and dress.'

They made it with barely a minute to spare, and were seated out on the terrace overlooking the bay.

Suzanne requested champagne, conferred with Sloane over the menu choices, and they opted for a light meal, preferring entrée servings with salads and fresh fruit.

The scallops mornay were superb, the oysters kilpatrick divine, and the prawns delectable.

They delighted in feeding each other morsels of food in a feast that equally fed their palates and their senses.

Anticipation was a powerful aphrodisiac, and they deliberately lingered, delaying the return to their villa by tacit consent.

There was background music, and Suzanne smiled as Sloane stood and held out his hand.

'You mentioned something about dancing.'

Heaven didn't get any better than this, she decided dreamily as she slipped into his arms. His hold was hardly conventional, and his lips grazed her temple, creating an evocative pattern that heated her blood to fever pitch.

It would be all too easy to whisper, Let's get out of here.

He sensed the moment she almost wavered, and brushed a kiss down the slope of her nose. There were other nights, a whole lifetime of them. He closed his eyes, then opened them again. *Thank God*, he thought in silent reverence.

Did she realise how much she meant to him? How the prospect of a life without her was akin to slowly dying?

He had known from the first moment they met that she was special. Courting her should have been easy. Never once had he even had to *try* with a woman. They were there for the taking, the selection entirely his. Suzanne had been different. There was no façade, no games, no emotional baggage. Just honesty, and a beautiful soul.

In retrospect, he acknowledged he'd moved too fast. The *image* of Wilson-Willoughby had proved to be a deterrent, for instead of enticing it had earned unaccustomed caution.

The night he'd walked into an empty penthouse and discovered she'd gone had been the worst night of his life. In the space of mere minutes he'd experienced very real fear, devastating loss, and a slow-mounting rage, the like of which he'd never known before. The note had left no phone number, no address, and no way of contacting her until eight-thirty the next morning when she arrived at the office.

'It's time to throw the bridal bouquet.'

He relaxed his hold and let her slip out from his arms, watching as she scooped up a display of frangipani and hibiscus from a nearby table centrepiece.

'To whom do you intend to throw it?'

'Ah, now there's a thing,' she said solemnly. 'The waiter? The waitress at the bar?'

All he had to do was raise his hand, murmur his request, and within minutes there were five staff members forming a line.

'It's not really a bouquet.'

'I don't think they'll care.'

They didn't, not at all, and she gave an infectious laugh as the flowers sailed a few metres and then separated easily between two pairs of hands.

Suzanne turned towards Sloane, and her eyes shone with mischief. 'Now we get to leave.'

There was a moon, bathing everything with a dim light, and halfway along the path she reached up and kissed him, only to gasp when he pulled her close and turned the impulsive gesture into something infinitely sensual.

They had almost an entire week of lazily spent days and long nights of lovemaking ahead of them, Suzanne reflected dreamily as they reached their villa. Time out for romance, before the return to reality in a cosmopolitan southern city and a faster pace of life.

Somehow their inevitable social obligations no longer seemed daunting.

Sloane unlocked the door, then switched on the light. Suzanne stepped inside, then came to an abrupt halt.

Inside, both downstairs and visible in the bedroom, grouped in vases, were masses of deep red roses, filling the villa with their delicate perfume.

She felt her eyes widen with sheer pleasure, then mist with the threat of tears. Slowly she turned to face him, her mouth shaky with emotion as she looked at him in silent query.

'While you were planning,' Sloane declared gently, 'I did a little planning of my own.'

'So many,' she said breathlessly, as she moved forward and touched a gentle finger to one velvet bud.

He crossed to stand behind her, curving her close into his body. His warm breath teased the hair at her temple as she sank back against him.

'A dozen to represent every year for the rest of our lives.'

Her heart seemed to turn over in her chest. She turned in his arms and reached up to link her hands together at his nape. His eyes were dark, so darkly gleaming she could almost see herself in their reflection.

'I love you. So much,' Suzanne whispered. 'I always have.'

His lips grazed hers, then lifted fractionally. 'I know,' he said gently. Her lips parted, and he pressed them closed. 'It was the only thing that kept me sane.'

His mouth closed over hers, seeking, finding every-thing she had to give and more, as he gave in return.

It wasn't enough, not nearly enough. Suzanne groaned as her fingers sought the hard flesh beneath his clothes, and she gasped as he swung an arm beneath her knees and lifted her high against his chest.

Her lips were slightly swollen, and her eyes deep and slumberous, as he strode towards the steps leading up to the bedroom.

'I am capable of walking,' she teased, and nearly died at the depth of passion evident in his gaze.

'Isn't the groom supposed to carry the bride over the threshold?'

'Something like that,' she said with mock serious-ness. She lifted a hand and trailed her fingers down the edge of his cheek. 'What other traditions do you have in mind?'

He reached the upper level, crossed to the large bed, and lowered her down to stand within the circle of his arms. 'One or two.'

His fingers freed the loops attaching two tiny but-tons at her nape, then he slid the zip fastening down the length of her back. The pale silk whispered to the floor to pool at her feet.

Soft opaque lining had negated the need to wear a bra, and she quivered beneath the intensity of his gaze, all too aware of her body's reaction. Only lace bikini briefs remained, and her eyes widened as he reached out a hand and extracted a single rose from a nearby vase.

With exquisite care he touched the velvet-petalled

bud to her cheek, then trailed it gently to the edge of her mouth.

The delicate scent teased her nostrils, and she felt all her fine body hairs rise in acute sensual expectation as he traced an evocative pattern to the valley between each breast.

Slowly, with infinite care, he gently outlined one breast, then the other, before trailing down to rest at her navel.

Suzanne's breath caught as desire arrowed through her body, igniting each erogenous zone in a conflagrant path and sending fire coursing through her veins.

With one deliberate movement he reached forward and pulled the covers from the bed, and she watched in mesmerised fascination as he lifted the rosebud to his lips.

Her eyes widened, dilating into huge pools of dark blue sapphire as he carefully peeled one petal free and let it flutter down on the bedsheets. Then another, and another, slowly, until only the rose stem and its stamen remained.

Suzanne thought her bones would melt, and a slow, sweet smile curved her generous mouth as she stepped out of her shoes.

She reached for the buttons on his shirt and undid them one by one, then discarded it. Her fingers moved to the buckle at his waist, dispensed with it, then she freed the zip fastening his trousers. Shoes and socks slid off easily.

Without a word she collected a rose, then, giving

his chest a gentle push, she tumbled him down onto the bed.

His husky laughter brought forth a wickedly teasing gleam and her eyes danced at the thought of what she had in store for him.

Mirroring his actions, she slowly peeled one petal and let it drift down onto his torso. Then another, and another, with infinite care, until there was none.

With a witching smile she reached forward and plucked another rose from a nearby vase, and gently placed it against his mouth.

Sloane doubted he would ever be able to look at a rose again without experiencing a damning and very intimate reaction. Petals softer than a woman's touch, their brush against sensitive skin incredibly evocative, the eroticism so intense it took all his will-power to lie supine while she conducted the sensual stroking. Much more of this...

Suzanne saw the instant his eyes darkened, and she gave a soft, throaty laugh as he pulled her down on top of him.

The rose slipped from her fingers and fell to the floor as he surged into her, and she reached for his forearms as he caught hold of her hips, commanding a ride that had no equal in her experience.

Moisture filmed her skin, his, as he took her to a place where control had no meaning and the senses exploded in a starburst of heat so intense she thought she might *burn* with it.

Afterwards she collapsed against his chest in a state of emotional exhaustion. She could feel the drift of his fingers against her skin as he caressed the indentations of her spine.

Gradually her breathing steadied, and her heart slowed to an even beat.

She wanted to stay close to him like this for ever. To feel, to know that their loving would always be so intense, so emotive. A true meshing of the emotions, physical, mental and spiritual.

Suzanne lifted her head and looked down into those dark, passion-filled eyes, and felt her body turn to jelly.

'I love you,' Sloane said with heartfelt simplicity. 'I know I couldn't survive a life without you in it. You're everything there is, and more. So much more.'

Tears filmed her eyes, and she lifted a hand to brush gentle fingers across his mouth. 'Same goes.'

He parted his teeth and nipped one finger, then drew it into his mouth and laved it with his tongue.

Awareness swirled into active life, spiralling through her body with damning ease, and she shifted slightly, exulting in the quickening power of his arousal as it swelled inside her.

In one smooth movement he rolled over and pinned her against the mattress.

The scent of crushed rose petals was strong, and she curved her legs around his hips, drawing him in close as she linked her hands together and pulled his head down to hers.

'Thank you.' She brushed his mouth with her own.

'For today. The roses. Everything. *You*, especially you.'

'My pleasure,' Sloane murmured against her lips, aware the pleasure was mutual. As it always would be.

Take 2 bestselling love stories FREE

Plus get a FREE surprise gift!

EXPECTING

She's sexy, she's successful... and she's pregnant!

Relax and enjoy these new stories about spirited women and gorgeous men, whose passion results in pregnancies... sometimes unexpectedly! All the new parents-to-be will discover that the business of making babies brings with it the most special love of all....

Harlequin Presents® brings you one **EXPECTING!** book each month throughout 1999.
Look out for:

The Baby Secret by Helen Brooks
Harlequin Presents #2004, January 1999

Expectant Mistress by Sara Wood
Harlequin Presents #2010, February 1999

Dante's Twins by Catherine Spencer
Harlequin Presents #2016, March 1999

Available at your favorite retail outlet.

HARLEQUIN®
Makes any time special ™

Passion

Looking for stories that *sizzle?*
Wanting a read that has a little extra *spice?*

Every other month throughout 1999,
Harlequin Presents® is thrilled to bring you
romances that turn up the heat!

Look out for:

The Seduction Project by **Miranda Lee**
Harlequin Presents #2003, January 1999

The Marriage Surrender
by **Michelle Reid**
Harlequin Presents #2014, March 1999

Marriage Under Suspicion
by **Sara Craven**
Harlequin Presents #2026, May 1999

*Pick up a **PRESENTS PASSION**—
where **seduction** is guaranteed!*

Available wherever Harlequin books are sold.

HARLEQUIN®
Makes any time special ™

HPPAS1

**For a limited time, Harlequin and Silhouette
have an offer you just can't refuse.**

In November and December 1998:

BUY **ANY** TWO HARLEQUIN
OR SILHOUETTE BOOKS and
SAVE $10.00
off future purchases

OR BUY ANY THREE HARLEQUIN OR SILHOUETTE BOOKS
AND **SAVE $20.00** OFF FUTURE PURCHASES!

(each coupon is good for $1.00 off the purchase of two
Harlequin or Silhouette books)

• •

JUST BUY 2 HARLEQUIN OR SILHOUETTE BOOKS, SEND US YOUR
NAME, ADDRESS AND 2 PROOFS OF PURCHASE (CASH REGISTER
RECEIPTS) AND HARLEQUIN WILL SEND YOU A COUPON BOOKLET
WORTH $10.00 OFF FUTURE PURCHASES OF HARLEQUIN OR
SILHOUETTE BOOKS IN 1999. SEND US 3 PROOFS OF PURCHASE AND
WE WILL SEND YOU 2 COUPON BOOKLETS WITH A TOTAL SAVING OF
$20.00. (ALLOW 4-6 WEEKS DELIVERY) OFFER EXPIRES
DECEMBER 31, 1998.

• •

I accept your offer! Please send me a coupon booklet(s), to:

NAME: _____

ADDRESS: _____

CITY: _____ STATE/PROV.: _____ POSTAL/ZIP CODE: _____

Send your name and address, along with your cash register
receipts for proofs of purchase, to:

In the U.S.	In Canada
Harlequin Books	Harlequin Books
P.O. Box 9057	P.O. Box 622
Buffalo, NY	Fort Erie, Ontario
14269	L2A 5X3

PHQ4982

Race to the altar—
Maxie, Darcy and Polly are

The **HUSBAND** *Hunters*

in a fabulous new
Harlequin Presents® miniseries by

LYNNE GRAHAM

These three women have each been left a share of
their late godmother's estate—but only if they marry
withing a year and remain married for six months....

Maxie's story: **Married to a Mistress**
Harlequin Presents #2001, January 1999

Darcy's story: **The Vengeful Husband**
Harlequin Presents #2007, February 1999

Polly's story: **Contract Baby**
Harlequin Presents #2013, March 1999

Will they get to the altar in time?

Available in January, February and March 1999
wherever Harlequin books are sold.

HARLEQUIN®
Makes any time special ™

Coming Next Month

HARLEQUIN PRESENTS®

THE BEST HAS JUST GOTTEN BETTER!

#2001 MARRIED TO A MISTRESS Lynne Graham
(The Husband Hunters)
If Maxie Kendall marries within a year, she'll inherit a fortune.
As she must clear her father's debts, she needs to find a
husband—*fast!* Greek tycoon Angelos Petronides definitely
wants to bed her...but will he want to wed her?

#2002 ONE NIGHT IN HIS ARMS Penny Jordan
Sylvie had been determined to act cool and distant for this
meeting with Ranulf Carrington—after all his cruel words last
time. But her body still ached for his...and Sylvie knew she'd
do almost anything for just one night in his arms....

#2003 THE SEDUCTION PROJECT Miranda Lee
(Presents Passion)
Molly's makeover hadn't succeeded in getting Liam Delaney
interested in her. It was time for an ultimatum. If Liam didn't
want her to lose her virginity to another admirer, he'd just
have to make love to her himself!

#2004 THE BABY SECRET Helen Brooks
(Expecting!)
Victoria's marriage had only lasted one night! It seemed
her husband, Zac, had a mistress—so Victoria had fled
immediately. But Zac had found her...and wasn't keen to
give her up. And he didn't even know about the baby yet....

#2005 THE PLAYBOY AND THE NANNY Anne McAllister
When a wealthy businessman offered Mari a job as a live-in
nanny, she wasn't expecting her charge to be a rebellious
thirty-two-year-old playboy! But Nikos Costanides didn't
want to be reformed...he wanted to seduce Mari!

#2006 A SUITABLE MISTRESS Cathy Williams
Dane Sutherland was rich, powerful and sinfully gorgeous. He
had it all—but he wanted more! He wanted Suzanne...and she
was equally determined not to fall into his arms...or his bed!